Rhys

A Question of Girls

Beatrice Holloway

First published in Great Britain in 2022
By TSL Publications, Rickmansworth

Copyright © 2022 Beatrice Holloway

ISBN: 978-1-915660-19-0

Cover :Photo https://pixabay.com/illustrations/young-woman-boy-sketch-drawing-6919498/

Dedication

Denis John
30.10.1927 - 19.12.2012

Hoping no one heard his gasp, Rhys quickly covered his mouth. If his best friend, Giddy, who, now they were nearly seventeen, preferred to be called, Idris, 'Because girls might get the wrong idea,' had heard, he knew he would be teased mercilessly. Giddy had got the nickname when in the Infant School. Every day, in the playground, he would spin himself round and round, faster and faster until he fell down, giddy and laughing. As it was, at the time of gasping Rhys also went very red in the face and there was an uncomfortable prickling under his arms.

'Come on,' yelled Idris across the shop floor, 'Stop day-dreaming. Let's get a move on.' Rhys knew what he meant especially as it was late in the afternoon. Idris was keen to get back to the mountain behind their Welsh village to rough ride their joint ownership of an ancient motorbike.

They had stopped at the local store to shop, Idris for cigarettes and Rhys for boiled sweets. He had decided not to take up smoking but was sometimes tempted and had a few sweets handy to ward off any desire to take up the habit. He had tried, just once, but choked and was laughed at, and vowed not to bother ever again.

All through their childhood they had been short of funds and even though both were now earning, cash was limited and the motorbike, was their joy and passion at the moment.

Rhys was an apprentice carpenter/joiner in town, whilst Idris, as he put it, 'A blessed apprentice of sorts to this bloke. Supposed to be teaching me plastering with very little pay for a lot of running about for him. A goffa that's me.' He grinned as he added, 'but the old dears we work for often slip me a bob or two and keep me in barra brith and Welsh cakes.'

Rhys had chosen his career, knowing that when he finished at the one-day a week college attendance, and being instructed and carefully monitored by whoever he was assigned too, he would probably never be out of work.

Giddy, however, after leaving school, had been at a loose end for weeks until one day, whilst kicking a can about in the street with other out-of-work youths, a van had pulled up beside them.

'Any of you lads, fancy a day's work? Just a bit of mixing up some plaster. Pay you well.' All the lads shook their heads, except Giddy.

He looked at the ground and put his hands in his pockets, pretending not to be really interested in the answer. 'What you paying?'

'Depends how much bloody effort you put into it lad.'

Giddy shrugged. 'I could give it a go, I suppose.'

'Hop aboard, lad, I'm late already.'

'Hang on a mo. You agree to pay me at the end of the day and bring me back here when we're done. Okay?'

'Oh get in. What do you think I was going to do? Abduct you or something. Buck up.' Giddy climbed in beside the man and shook his hand. And so began Giddy's apprenticeship.

The bike they purchased, was a 1960's Royal Enfield. Its top speed was reputed to be over a hundred miles per hour, but the best they could get was around sixty and at that speed, the bike had begun to shudder. They had taken it apart, laying out each component, as Idris's father had shown them so that putting it back together would not cause a problem. Needless to say, there were many problems, but after a few weekends, it was clean and running. It was Idris who decided what he thought was a fair share of the driving. 'Tell you what, Ree. You have it Monday to Friday, that way you can go to work later, you'll not have to wait for the bus.'

'And ...? 'There was a slyness in Idris's answer.

'That means I shall have it Saturday and Sunday!' There was some sense in the suggestion.

But, Rhys thought, as he paid for his sweets, the motorbike

was a means of transport for the weekends as well; for a trip to the sea or a visit to a club, even watch a rugby match any distance from home.

'So you can go off gallivanting leaving me to use the bus or walk. I think not, butt.'

'Now, you know I wouldn't do that to you, we're always together most weekends. We can go to places together, but me driving.' And so it was agreed, an agreement that sometimes Rhys regretted, especially when Idris tried some daring tricks while he was a passenger clinging on the back.

Rhys raised his hand and called back to Idris, 'Just getting my change.' He turned, but what had caused his earlier, brief, consternation had gone. Gone was the *tylwyth teg*, the elf whose chestnut hair glinted in the sunlight as it swung across her shoulders when her laughing face lifted towards the young man talking to her. He felt a brief moment of regret, knowing somehow that it was a special moment.

All thoughts of the girl were gone when sitting astride the motorbike behind Idris, who was impatient to get to the mountain.

'Did you know it is only twenty miles per hour in the village?' he yelled in Idris's ear.

The answer he got was, 'It's thirty, you silly blighter.'

Leaning over Idris's shoulder to check the speedometer, Rhys shouted back, 'So why are you doing forty-eight?' They slowed down immediately, Idris prudently remembered PC Hughes had said last time he had been caught speeding through the village, 'I told you last week, if I catch you just once more above the speed limit lad, I'll see to it that you lose your license. Understand?'

And Idris had replied rather cheekily, 'Have a heart officer, I was only two miles above the limit.'

'More like twenty-two by my reckoning. Go on, clear off, and remember, this is your very last warning.' Idris knew the officer meant every word this time, even though he had a reputation of being a bit of a softy. The warning meant he could be fined or even lose his license if caught again. As far as he was concerned, there would be nothing left in life for him without his weekend jaunts on the bike. Rhys sighed with relief, especially as they were now in his gran's street. He saw her in her garden and raise her head as she heard the bike roar into the area. As they sped by he raised his hand and called out, 'See you, gran. Only doing twenty-nine. Ok?' He knew she would be tutting and telling him off when he next visited, and he wasn't even driving.

Once they had reached the bottom of the Pen-y-Bryn, the local mountain, and the playground of their childhood, they made their way to the top. To do this they had to alternate between walking and pushing the bike and where the ground was easier, jumping back onto the vehicle. There was a group of motorcyclists waiting for them, anxious to start their weekly challenges. That was, to reach the bottom of the mountain, in the fastest time, finding the easiest route, and disqualification if the rider fell. Falls were quite common, especially after rain that made the loose scree more slippery and dangerous. Most of the lads were familiar with the terrain, and these tests seemed now to be too easy.

Today there was to be a difference. Instead of just the rider participating, they had to ferry a pillion passenger down as well. Apart from helmets, most of the participants had little or no safety clothing. Injuries had been light so far, no one needing medical care. Almost all had at one time or another scraped their elbows and knees but no one was ever deterred by their injuries and turned up as usual the following Saturday.

Francis was the timekeeper as his watch had a seconds hand and he also clapped two stones together to start the race. The racer had to sound his horn when he reached the bottom of the mountain. This was confirmed by another lad stationed at the end of the route. With mixed feelings Rhys climbed onto the seat behind his friend. Rhys could see that Giddy was excited, anticipating the ride down and no doubt, prepared to take chances.

'You on?' Giddy questioned. Not waiting for an answer, he went on, 'Don't yell in my ear, trust me will you?'

'As long as you don't do anything daft, just remember I'm on the back.'

'You softy,' jeered Giddy.

'Bet you wouldn't like to be the pillion rider.'

'With you driving! We'd never get there.' This remark got Giddy a resounding thump in the back.

'You two ready?' the timekeeper intervened.

Together they answered, 'Yes' and the stones were immediately clapped together. Giddy was not pleased, he had been caught unready. The engine had already been running for a few moments, and after swearing at the grinning starter, he twisted the throttle until it roared loudly and shot off down the course. The momentum caused Rhys to sway backwards then shoot forward. Clinging onto the steel saddlebag holder behind him, he shouted, 'Don't forget I'm on the back you idiot.'

It was if Giddy hadn't heard him. He leaned dangerously close to the ground going round corners, hardly checking his speed and ignoring the fact that the corner might lead straight into another tight corner. He almost stood up when going over uneven ground and he braked hard, too hard. By now, Rhys was experiencing an adrenaline rush and was sure Giddy was as well. There was, too, a modicum of fear but the exhilaration of speed countered this.

They were just over halfway down the mountainside when disaster struck. There was a short straight run of a few yards, and taking advantage of this, Giddy, face alive with exhilaration, slightly turned his head to shout, 'We're going to make it!' Lacking concentration for one nanosecond brought about disaster for the two boys. A small rivulet trickled over the track, and the wheels slid then lost purchase crossing the water. The bike swung around, throwing the boys off. Fortunately, Giddy had his helmet on as his head hit a hidden rock as he fell then slid a few yards down the gravelly route. Rhys tumbled first into the water then into some brambles. For a few moments both boys lay still, then Rhys let his temper rip. 'You bloody idiot!' As there was no immediate reply, he anxiously and more in control, enquired, 'Giddy?' The answer he got was a groan. Giddy was known to exaggerate, but this groan sounded serious. 'Giddy? You all right?'

'Give us hand, will you?'

Rhys rolled over onto his knees, then carefully stood up. There were ugly scratches along both arms, his elbow hurt and he had torn his jeans. Through the tear, blood was gently oozing from a gash. He also realised that his tee shirt was wet and clung coldly against his body. By this time the other riders were beside them. They hauled Giddy up who was holding his neck. Between them, they ferried both Rhys and Idris to the A&E Department.

At the hospital, after cleaning and applying antiseptic cream to his scratches, told he only had bruises to his elbow and finally a couple of stitches to his, not so bad, cut on his thigh, Rhys was discharged. He made his way to the cubicle where Giddy lay, he too had been cleaned up. Although his friction burns were superficial he was to stay in hospital overnight in case the bump to his head caused trouble. Both boys were reprimanded for not having the right gear for motorcycling. With folded arms and a stern expression, the doctor said, 'It is essential to wear protective clothing. A proper leather jacket to start with, trousers too, proper boots and gauntlets or leather gloves.'

The two boys looked at each other, before Giddy answered, 'Some hopes.'

From a public phone in the hospital waiting room, now busy as it was late Saturday evening, Rhys telephoned his brother, Emlyn, to come and collect him and take him home.

Emlyn, who once had a motorcycle and now had a car in order to ferry his growing family said little on the journey home. On opening the door, and aimed at Rhys, they were greeted with, 'Where have you been? Your dinner's cold. You should have let us know if you're going to be late,' his angry mother called out.

Her tone changed immediately she saw Rhys. 'Good Lord, whatever's happened? That motorbike I guess. Just look at you.' As she was saying this, she was plumping up cushions in his father's favourite armchair, and reaching out to guide him to it. Once he was settled, she put the kettle on. 'Sweet tea's good for shock,' she said. 'And that's what you're getting. Then perhaps you can manage your dinner. I kept it hot.'

Emlyn, preparing to leave, told Rhys, 'I'll get the bike later and bring it round tomorrow.'

Rhys sighed, and before the tea was in his hand he was asleep. The last thing he heard, was his father saying, 'That damn bike's got to go.'

Rhys woke late the next morning in his own bed. He vaguely remembered being pushed and pulled up the stairs by his father and brother who must also have also undressed him down to his underwear. The various aches and pains he experienced as he attempted to get out of bed, reminded him of yesterday. Then his thoughts turned to Giddy. Immediately, he decided to have a bath, and was surprised to see rainbow hues of bruises on his body that he hadn't noticed before. Once dressed, he dashed downstairs and was greeted by his mother.

'So, you're up at last. I'll get you some breakfast. What do you fancy?'

'Just a cup of tea, will do. I got to go round to Giddy's. Got to see how he's doing.' He looked at his mother as she stood with her arms akimbo on her hips. The tone of her voice alerted him to a lecture coming up. He was right.

'Ever since you were lads, that boy has got you into more trouble than, than ...' She was momentarily lost for words. 'Than a cartload of monkeys. There was time when you and him ...' She hesitated, 'Well, I won't go on, but it was because of that boy that I was called up to the school a thousand times.' She turned to the stove and banged the frying pan down on the hob. 'And, my lad, there was a constant stream of neighbours complaining.' She shrugged her shoulders and sniffed, 'Not that I took much notice, mind.' She threw some rashers into the pan and as they sizzled, buttered slices of bread to make his favourite sarnie.

A few minutes later she passed him a mug of tea and a full plate of sandwiches. As she put them in front of him she ruffled his hair. 'There now, get that lot inside you.' Washing up the dishes at the sink she turned and smiled at him. 'We did get some peace when you both went to different schools, now ...' she sighed, 'seems like trouble is going to visit us again.'

As soon as the door was opened when Rhys arrived at Giddy's house he was greeted by his mother. 'I thought it might be you, and yes he's home no thanks to you.'

'But ...' he began.

'But what?' she snapped.

Both heard Giddy call out, 'That you Rhys? Come on up.'

His mother sighed, 'I reckon you two must be joined at the hip. It's time you both sorted yourselves out. Go your own ways. Nothing but mayhem when my boy's with you, Rhys Evans. Nearly killed him this time didn't you? I should have banned you from your infant days. 'A really bad influence you are, to be sure.'

Rhys was very indignant at these remarks, knowing who was to blame, but he didn't say. Like his mother, she probably wouldn't believe him anyway. 'But Mrs Cooper ...' he began again.

She opened the door wider. 'Well you'd better go up, I suppose. I'll get no peace if I send you off with a flea in your ear,' and stood aside for him to enter.

Sitting up in bed, Rhys saw at once the bandaged head and various plasters on his friend's face and arms. He also noticed Giddy was tucking into a bowl of chocolate ice cream.

Giddy chortled. 'Did she have a go at you? She's convinced you made me do it.'

Rhys, with a grin on his face, nodded.

'Well, you should have put her right. I told you it was dangerous.'

'Aw! Come on. You enjoyed it just as much as I did. And anyway, what's a few scratches?' He spooned some ice cream into his mouth and added, 'mind you, being waited on with special foods and lots of petting ain't so bad. Well worth it.'

'I'll not bother, thank you.'

Mrs Cooper came into the room. 'Well I'll not have you

stealing his treats as well, Rhys Evans,' she said as she handed him a large helping of ice cream and a spoon.

'Thank you, I must say I was tempted, but your poorly invalid might have hit me.' He was pleased to see she tried to hide her smile as she left.

'See,' said Giddy. 'She's not so bad as a mum. Don't take any notice of what she says about you.'

Rhys laughed and spluttered ice cream across the bed sheets as he replied, 'I don't, and for your information, my mother says exactly the same about you.' They grinned at each other as they tried to clean up the sheet until they realised they were making it ten times worse, gave up and continued tucking into their treat.

Wiping his mouth and sighing, Giddy asked, 'How's the bike? Busted no doubt.'

'Don't think so. Em's going to bring it round this afternoon. If there's anything wrong, he'll fix it. He's good at that sort of thing. Remember, he got an old one from the army years ago and got that going. Went on for ages until he bought a car.'

'Call that a car? It's an old banger.'

'I know, but it gets him and his kids around.' He was quiet for a moment then, 'Anyway, I hope he offers to get me to work tomorrow morning. If not, I'll have to get up early to get the quarter to seven bus.'

Giddy said nothing as he knew one of Rhys's faults was that he was a reluctant riser.

After an hour or so, and seeing his friend was really not too badly injured after yesterday's event, Rhys said his goodbyes and made his way downstairs. As he reached the street door, Mrs Cooper called out, 'Mark my words, Rhys just one more time you get my boy in trouble and I guarantee you will truly regret it!' He didn't reply.

The first thing he saw in his backyard when he reached home, was the rather battered motorbike. He stroked a loving hand over the petrol tank and smiled to himself, Emlyn will fix it, he thought. In the kitchen his brother, father and mother were sitting at the table enjoying a cup of tea. From the oven came the smell of the Sunday lunch roast.

'Here he is,' said his father. 'Tell him the worst, Em. there's a good lad.'

Rhys's heart sank as he joined them at the table – his mother had already jumped up and poured him a drink. Emlyn winked at him before saying, 'Probably not as much damage to the bike as there is to you and Giddy, Rhys. Won't take long to fix, but can't do anything until Wednesday, my day off.'

'Okay, thanks,' he replied, but his heart sank at the thought of the two mornings' early rise.

'It might cost a bob or two. I'll get what's needed, but you'll have to pay me back quick or the kids will go hungry.' He smiled as he said this, seeing their dad nodding approval, but Rhys knew his brother was only joking.

'No problem, but be as quick as you can won't you? I especially need it for this weekend.'

'What?' bellowed Dad. 'No way, my son, that bike's going as soon as it's fixed. You're not risking your life on that clapped-out bit of machinery ever again. Do you hear me?'

Rhys saw Emlyn shake his head, 'Steady on Dad. By the time I've finished with it, it will be fit for a king. And how's the lad going to get about? You won't want to run him to work and back every day, take him to the discos at the weekend, then collect him at two in the morning. He's got to have wheels to ...'

'Then he can save up for a modest car – a three-wheeler like Delboy's on the telly. You know the programme I mean?'

'*Only Fools and Horses*, Yer, I know it. Their car is worse than the bike! Won't go faster than twenty miles an hour at best!'

'And that would suit his mother and me fine.'

Turning to Rhys, Emlyn said, 'I'll pick you up in the

morning and Tuesday. This is the only time I'm going to help you out. You got to sort yourself out somehow, Rhys. Half-past seven tomorrow then. Should just about get you in on time.'

'How you going to manage that?' their father asked.

Giving a wink to Rhys, Em relied, 'Someone owes me.'

There was a wide grin on Rhys's face as he gave his heartfelt thanks. Em's offer meant that he wouldn't lose a couple of days pay, nor would he get a good telling off from Mr Bert, his mentor, who would include his favourite saying, 'Yer arms and legs not broken so you can get on with it.' There might also have been a heavy lecture from the Governor, but best of all, no need to get up early was a definite bonus.

True to his word, Emlyn worked hard on the motorbike on Wednesday. He was a milkman. Although milk doorstep delivery was dying out in towns with easy access to supermarkets, in the Welsh countryside, the service was still in full force. Emlyn enjoyed his work, making a start at five in the morning when the roads were empty except for newspaper boys, sometimes the bin lorry and at weekends, sometimes bleary-eyed revellers. Rhys was delighted to see the vehicle upright on its new stands, a new silver coloured exhaust pipe and the petrol tank cleaned with the enamel motif firmly fixed in place.

'Well,' said Emlyn, 'what do you think?'

Rhys, with a huge grin on his face, thanked his brother, then suggested a spin around the village to make sure everything was in working order.

'Cheeky devil. 'Of course it's working,' and promptly sat astride the bike. 'Coming?' Rhys, a little miffed as he wanted to try it out for himself, climbed on behind. Em started up the engine and twisting the throttle on the handlebar making the engine roar, yelled above the noise, 'Sounds good, doesn't it?' They had a quick trip around the village, tooting as they passed their grandparents' house and finally filling up the petrol tank.

'Right then,' began Emlyn when they returned to the garden to gather up his tools, 'You can pay me back by babysitting on Saturday. Okay?'

Although a little dismayed, but knowing he and Giddy had no definite plans for the weekend – yet – Rhys, nodded and asked, 'What time then?'

'Not sure yet, I'll let you know.'

Rhys hoped that the two children would be in bed, even

though he had a soft spot for Charlotte, his eldest niece.

At work the following day, he was greeted with, 'Been in the war son?' and before Rhys could say a word, Mr Bert pointed towards one of the new houses, and said, 'Go and help George with the floorboards over there.' Rhys preferred working alongside Mr Bert who had taken him under his wing over a year ago. With only a few tools his granddad and dad had found in their sheds, Rhys was a bit overwhelmed on his first day as an apprentice. He'd chosen to become a carpenter/ joiner when one of the school masters had told him that he had a natural aptitude working with wood. As time went on, Rhys appreciated his mentor more and more, the other apprentice starting the same day was not so lucky, as Rhys had witnessed the lad being clouted more than once for minor errors. Mr Bert would have teased him a bit calling him a damn fool or suchlike, then show Rhys where he had gone wrong and how to put it right. It was a long day, the aches he still had from Saturday's event didn't help as he crawled about the floor bashing floorboards he had carried up a ladder then nailed into place, the work was repetitive and brain numbing boring, all done working alongside unsympathetic George.

Thursdays were the best of the working days as it was the day he attended college. The small company he worked for had agreed to allow him to attend.

It was on the Saturday morning milk round when Emlyn called in to his mother's asking for Rhys. It was nearly ten o'clock and he was still in bed. As he put it, 'A growing lad needs plenty of rest.' His mother's calling up the stairs, eventually roused him.

'Rhys, Em's here, wants a word with you.'

Rhys groaned, and turned over, ready to settle down again, so answered, 'Tell him I'll phone him later.'

'Get down here, you lazy blighter, pronto,' his brother shouted. 'I need to talk to you. Hurry, or I'll be late on my round.'

Rubbing his face, yawning, then stretching, Rhys entered the kitchen. Immediately, his mother chided, 'Where's your dressing gown? You'll catch your death of cold like that.' She made for the stairs when he didn't turn back to get it. 'Stay there, talk to Emlyn, I'll get it,' she sighed.

Sitting down heavily onto a chair, Rhys picked up the newspaper that was immediately snatched out of his hand. 'Oi!' he spluttered, 'I was reading that.'

'No you weren't, you were trying to avoid hearing what I'm going to say.'

'Which is?'

'Today is our wedding anniversary and me and Megan fancy a night out, so you're on mate, babysitting.'

Two things crossed Rhys's mind. First he thought, 'Oh no.' Then secondly, 'Might as well get it over so I don't owe anything.' He shrugged.

'So, what time, then?'

Emlyn gave a sigh of relief, he thought he might have had to argue, but everything was fine. 'I'm booking a meal for half past six.'

'That's early.'

'Yes, but you forget I have to be up at five, even on a Sunday. I want to be in bed by half past nine at the latest.'

'I'll be there. Will the kids be in bed?'

'Not that early, but Megan will have given them their tea, and got them ready for bed. And I mean bed, Rhys, half past seven at the latest, no larking about.'

'Me? Larking about? What gives you that idea?' there was a certain amount of innocence in this questioning. Emlyn, laughed.

'I know you too well, boyo. You wind them up and it's the devil's own job to settle them. Me and Megan, would just like to come home and have a quiet few hours on our own.'

Their mother had returned and as Rhys put on his dressing

gown, she said, 'I can sit for you, if you like.'

'Thanks Mam, but Rhys owes me, and anyway it will do him good have some time with the children.' At this, both saw her raise her eyebrows and shake her head.

'It's alright, Mam. I'll do it. Be fun to be with them for a bit.'

Emlyn, took a bottle of milk out of his crate and put it on the table. 'There Mam, the best, lots of cream on the top.' Turning to Rhys, who had begun reading the paper again, he said, 'No later than quarter past six, Rhys, right?' Rhys, didn't reply, but nodded.

Saturday, and at six o'clock Rhys stood in the doorway of Emlyn's kitchen looking at his charges for the evening. They were both in their pyjamas, with clean, shiny faces, sitting at the table finishing their supper. Charlotte, nearly seven years old, was, in his opinion a pretty child with blue eyes, that when they gazed at you in innocence, you just knew she was planning some mischief. He loved that about her, and was often part of her conspiracies. She was a little plump, and he teased her by calling her Dumpling. In retaliation, she would call him Spindle shanks, an old-fashioned word for someone who was very thin. Usually, he called her Charlie, the name he had insisted on when she was a few weeks old, and had instructed her to behave like a boy if they were to be friends.

Five years old David was her brother, although to look at them together you would find it hard to believe they were siblings. Where Charlie was fair in skin and hair, David was the opposite, dark eyes with almost black hair that tumbled around his face. Rhys had learned some time ago that if David was quiet, David was up to mischief, that often equalled that of his approving sister.

As soon as the children saw him, they launched themselves at him, David clinging to his legs as he caught Charlie and threw her up into the air before catching her. Both began chattering, David telling him about his lovely teacher, his drawings and the awful school dinners. Charlie's news included her new dancing lessons, Rhys sighed inwardly knowing she was going to be 'girly', but then he conceded, why not, now that he had found girls interesting. He knew already, that babysitting tonight was going to be a challenge, almost wishing that the pair didn't exist. Ruefully, he admitted to himself that yes, he did love them and woe betide anyone who dared to upset them.

Megan bustled into the kitchen. 'Now then, Rhys, the children are to be in bed by seven-thirty. You can tell them a story, nothing too exciting or they'll not settle and not give you any peace. Understand?'

Rhys nodded, but winked at the children.

With a stern face she turned to Charlie and David, 'I mean it, bed by seven-thirty and no nonsense.'

Emlyn called out from the open front door, 'Come on Meg, we'll be late. The table's booked and I'm gasping for a pint.' Megan, bent down and kissed both the children, wagged her finger at them and said, 'Be good.'

Always, the children knew that if Rhys had a bag, there would be some sort of surprise for them. As soon as the door closed behind their parents, they tried to wrestle the bag from Rhys, then jumping up when he held it high above his head. 'Sit down, you lot,' he was laughing, and a little out of breath trying to avoid them. They sat down, wriggling their little bodies in anticipation. Rhys put his hand into the bag. They watched as he pulled out a packet of?

'What have we got here?' There was a big surprise in Rhys's voice. 'Well I never!' he exclaimed as he showed them a bag of corn grains, just waiting to be cooked and smothered in sugar. It didn't take long to locate a suitable saucepan, he let the children pour all the seeds into the pan, then put the lid on it. He gave out the rules to them, he was in charge of the cooker, and they had to take turns to shake the pan every minute or so. It wasn't long before the first pop and the children began shouting and laughing. Shaking and popping, shaking and popping, until when it was his turn to shake, David, decided to take the lid off. An explosion of white, crinkled popcorn covered the cooker and surrounding work surfaces. 'Oh David! Who's going to clear all that up?' sighed Rhys. Before replacing the lid and returning the pan to the cooker, he allowed Charlie to add a generous, large spoon of sugar to the pan. Needless to say, she did this with a shaky hand, so that some fell onto the floor and crunched underfoot. Soon there was a lovely smell, something like toffee as the shaking and popping began again. When there were no more sounds from the pan, Rhys took off the lid. He sent the children to sit on the sofa then served each of them a generous helping on a sheet of kitchen paper. He was a little dismayed to see a great deal of burnt sugar on the bottom of the pan. When they had finished, Rhys noticed that sticky fingermarks were on the arms of the furniture. Oh! Well, he thought, once the pair were in bed, he would clean up the kitchen and sponge the furniture.

'What are we going to do now, Uncle Rhys?'

Rhys fished deeper into his bag and pulled out some wood off-cuts he was allowed from work. With a few crayons he let the children colour them as they wished, knowing that Em would be glad of the blocks for the fire later. He looked at the clock and said to the children, 'A story, I think, look it's nearly bedtime. What shall it be?'

'No, no, no. We want a game.'

Charlie peered up into Rhys's face, 'Pleeeeeease,' she begged. How could he resist?

'Oh, alright. Just one game of Islands. Get the cushions on the floor. Remember, the floor is a swamp, so if you touch the floor, you're out and you've got to keep moving.' Of course, the cushions were not the only safe refuge, so was the table, and chairs and sofas. And so the game began. The children, getting more and more excited, climbed and scrambled over every piece of furniture in the room, until they were exhausted. After a short rest they began again, but were interrupted by the door bell ringing. It was Giddy. Rhys had agreed to meet him later that evening, thinking they might go for a ride and probably a drink.

'Came early to see if you needed any help,' Giddy said. At just past eight o'clock, David was riding on Giddy's back, who was crawling around the room and neighing like a horse, and Charlie was being tickled by Rhys and giggling.

'BED, NOW,' Emlyn's voice boomed around the room. The two children squeezed round their parents in the doorway, making sure their bottoms were well away from the threat of a smack, then scuttled up the stairs as fast as they could.

Emlyn was furious. 'If they are not settled in ten minutes, you can take them home with you. You'll see what's it's like not to get a decent night's sleep.'

'Aw, come on Em...' Rhys began. 'We were just having a bit of fun, they loved it. They didn't miss you at all.' Megan had wandered into the kitchen, and needless to say, was pretty cross at the chaotic state she found.

'And when you bring them back in the morning, you can clean up the mess in the here,' she added.

Giddy mumbled to Rhys, 'Come on, let's get out of here before they mean it,' and grabbing their coats, they made a fast exit as Em's angry voice called after them, 'I won't forget this Rhys Evans, you wait and see.'

Rhys was always pleased when Thursday, College day, came round. On this particular Thursday, the morning had been spent on materials, including the identifying of woods, their density and uses. Also included was, yet again, safety guidance on the worksite and using tools with respect, especially those that relied on electricity, as the tools were faster needing precise control, and without care could be dangerous.

The morning ended with each student being asked to make a drawing of what they wanted to make in the workshop, a project to be completed by the end of term for an exhibition. They were cautioned that there were limited materials and time, and the work should include dovetail joints cut by hand. Rhys decided to make a small stationery box with a drawer.

At lunchtimes Rhys always asked for egg and chips and his plate was always piled high as he was a favourite with the counter staff. The other lads complained, saying he had more chips than they had and teased him. Rhys was sure this wasn't true, their plates all seemed the same to him. Half laughing he told his friends it was his charm and good manners, and they swore too much and too often. 'I reckon you bribe them,' someone said, and another was sure it was his watery eyes and they pitied him. Rhys ignored this last jibe, he was told often enough by his mother and gran that he had the most beautiful blue eyes that would send the ladies wild.

Usually, after lunch, the lads went to the waste ground to kick a ball around, but today it was raining. Some sat on desks to chat and smoke, and others, including Rhys, strolled about the college corridors, meeting and chatting with other students on different courses. As usual for these enforced indoor activities, they made their way to the Art Studios, one of the popular disciplines chosen by girls. It wasn't long before there was a mixed crowd of laughing, teasing, jostling and flirting students. One of the lads from the Art Department began calling to the girls that artists were better and more gentle lovers than the louts they were talking to could ever be. The would-be carpenter/joiner apprentices raised their eyebrows and grinned at each other. One of them, Adrian, turned to the girls, 'Anyone want to test out their theory?' he asked. The girls laughed, but one of the lads scowled and stepped towards Adrian as if looking for a fight.

'Steady on,' said Adrian, 'Only joshing.'

'These are our girls,' was the reply.

'What!' screamed a girl, 'Not a wimp like you for sure.'

'Shut your mouth, Iris. I was talking to this mob.' The so-called mob had had enough.

Very quietly and dangerously, Adrian said, 'But we have more respect for them.'

The rest of the lads looked at the challenger, and saw someone, who indeed, looked like a wimp. Someone who, of no real weight, was wearing heavy eye make-up, had dyed his hair and was wearing a psychedelic shirt. All of this effort did not quite meet the artistic image he was trying to achieve. The lads could see he was trying to disguise his trembling as he realised he had, perhaps, gone too far. There was a hurried short chat between the boys, then, 'Right lads,' said one. 'Let's have him,' and laughing, three boys pinned the trouble-maker's arms, at the same time avoiding his legs scrabbling in the air as between them they lifted him into a large waste bin nearby, then hoisted the bin plus occupant onto the top of a stationery cupboard.

It was nearly time for the afternoon sessions to begin, the girls wandered towards the studio, laughing and looking over their shoulders back at the prisoner. The lads too, moved on, not once looking back as they chuckled at the fellow's dilemma, who had begun shouting for help and threatening them at the same time.

It was as they were passing the Engineering workshop that Rhys saw some movement from the corner of his eye. He couldn't believe what he saw. He stopped suddenly, causing the lad behind him to crash into him. 'Plonker!' he said as he edged around Rhys. There she was, the girl he saw a few weeks ago in the sweet shop. Today she was dressed in overalls and was in the process of twisting her long shining hair into a rope and pinning it to the top of her head.

'Clear off, pervert,' she yelled at him.

'I, I ...' stuttered Rhys wanting to tell her he had seen her before. From nowhere, two boys appeared.

'You alright, Helen?' one asked and looking at Rhys, the other said, 'You heard, clear off. Now!'

Rhys didn't hesitate, he would be late if he didn't, but as he left, he smiled to himself, now he knew her name and she was here in the college. What's more, he thought as he entered the workshop, I'll make the box extra special for Helen, he would wax it and polish it so that it could be treasured, even perhaps an heirloom.

Nearly every day after school Rhys would visit his grand-parents, knowing there was always a welcome and some sort of treat – usually something home-baked. When he went to High School, it was a little more difficult to visit, but, without a doubt, he always called in if he had good news. Something trickier that might disappoint or cause trouble at home, it was to his grandparents' house he went to first. They rarely judged him, and always seemed to come up with some sort of compromise to get him, if not out of trouble, at least advice to soften the situation.

Starting work meant that the visits were fewer. He planned to visit every Sunday, but it often turned out that after a Saturday night out with Giddy, he often overslept, and by the time he'd bathed, had lunch, and prepared for work the next day, and as always, meeting up with Giddy in the evening, time for visiting the folk had gone.

This Sunday he had news to impart. News he didn't want to share with his parents, especially his mother, who would ask endless questions he knew he couldn't answer. Since Thursday, he had thought endlessly about Helen, even smiling to himself, and knew he had to be careful as at dinner that evening, coming around from such a daydream, he saw his parents exchanging looks, that implied, 'Something's up with the boy'. Nor did he want to confide in Giddy, who, he was certain, would tease him mercilessly. It was alright for Giddy, thought Rhys, he seemed to have a different girl every couple of weeks or so. He cheered up by telling himself that it was the girls who gave him the heave-ho. Not Giddy's casual offering, of 'She wasn't my type.' Yes, he thought Giddy was not any girl's dream - yet.

'Anyone home,' he called out as he opened his nan's back door. In no time at all, Nan had boiled the kettle, made a pot of tea and loaded a plate of Welsh cakes onto a tray.

'Take that into the parlour where Granddad is sitting toasting himself as usual in front of the fire, there's a good chap,' she said.

Once they had all settled with drinks, granddad, with his mouth full of cake, asked, 'So, how's it going lad? How's the job turning out?'

Rhys happily described his work and the men he was working with. As he reached for another Welsh cake, and turning to hide the sly grin on his face, he said, 'By the way, Granddad, I read in the local paper, that everyone collecting their pension on Tuesday will be given a can of beer. I thought you'd like to know.'

'Are you sure? Sounds a bit fishy to me.'

'Well, that's what I read.'

Granddad looked closely at Rhys, not sure if he was joking. After a moment, he said, 'Hmm. Could be. Election coming up in the spring, I reckon it's the government, bribing pensioners for their vote.' He turned to his wife, 'I'll get the pensions next week, Mrs. If it's true, I'll enjoy the drink more than you, aye, and I can have yours as well.'

'You! Prepared to wait half an hour or more in a queue. Well, that I must see.'

Rhys, keeping an innocent expression on his face, watched Granddad closely, and could see he was still unsure whether to believe him or not.

'A free can of beer, can't be bad, can it? But if you're telling porkies lad, just watch out, that's all I'm saying. Mark my words.'

'Granddad! Would I lie to you?'

Nan poured out second cups of tea for the menfolk, Granddad reached for his pipe and Rhys helped himself to another cake.

At last Nan asked the question that Rhys had been expecting, the question he always dreaded, one that she asked every time on his few visits. But today, he was happy as he had an answer for her.

'So, Rhys love, have you got yourself a young lady friend yet?'

He swallowed the last mouthful of cake and reached for his cup. He felt himself going red and hoped Nan didn't notice. Shyly, he said, 'Yes, Nan, I have. Met her at college.'

Nan gave a satisfied sigh. 'At last young man.' She settled herself comfortably on the sofa and patted the space beside her. 'Come on love, let's hear all about her.'

Granddad gave a snort and tapped out the ash from his pipe into the grate. 'You women, all the same. Want to know everyone's business. Don't take any notice of her son. She'll know when you are good and ready to tell.'

'Well, you just mind your own business, then,' Nan retorted. 'Now Rhys, is she pretty?' she began.

There was a broad grin on Rhys's face as he knew he could talk freely about his new found girlfriend. Well, he told himself, Helen could soon be, better still, he told himself sternly, will be my girlfriend. Just saying her name made him happy. 'Oh, yes, Nan, indeed she is very pretty. Comes up to my shoulder and smiles a lot.' He didn't mention that the last time he saw she had oil smudges on her face. Nor did he say she had a fiery disposition.

'So, what is her name? Where does she live? Have you met her family yet?'

'Wow, old girl,' Granddad cautioned. 'Give the lad a chance, he's only just met her, haven't you, lad?'

'That's right Granddad. 'Well, I've seen her twice, so far.' He turned towards his Nan, 'And her name is Helen.'

'You've had a date already! Where did you go?'

'Not yet, Nan. I met her at college and we said a few words to each other. Next week, I'll ask her out.'

'Where will you go? Pictures is always nice. There's some really good romantic films about at the moment, and you can hold hands in the dark.'

Granddad gave a grunt. 'So whose hand were you holding in the dark then Mrs, I'd like to know?' Nan shook her head.

'Take no notice, love, he knows full well whose hand it was.'

'His I suppose,' laughed Rhys.

'Well now, boy, I'm warning you. Be careful when you're courting this girl.'

'What do you mean, granddad? I won't be taking her out on the motorbike, got to get my license first, if that's what you mean.'

'You know what I'm saying. We don't want any...' Granddad hesitated, seeking for the right word. '...any unfortunate accidents, do we? You're far too young for any sort of shenanigans like that.'

Rhys felt himself going hot, then he half-smiled to himself. 'Granddad, are you talking about the birds and bees?' Granddad nodded.

'That's what I'm saying. Now you understand!'

Nan was outraged, and strode across to her husband and slapped him hard on his arm.

'You,' she said, 'just mind your own business. Rhys is all grown up now, no need to treat him like he was still eleven.'

Granddad, rubbed his arm, pretending she had hurt him. 'No need to get upset, my lady. Just trying to put the boy right.'

'He knows! Now leave him be.'

'Oh, alright. Just be careful, Rhys, that's all I'm saying.'

'Granddad,' there was a serious tone in Rhys's voice, at the same time trying to suppress the urge to laugh out loud. 'They can't make things to fit the birds and bees, that's why there's so many of them. We humans got more sense.'

It took a moment or two for Granddad to understand what had been said. Then, 'You cheeky little b...'

'Don't you go a swearing now,' warned Nan, but in a few moments all three were laughing.

It was Tuesday and it had been raining all day. Rhys had been held up in traffic on his way home in the evening, and as he sat astride the bike, he got wetter and wetter. He was so relieved be home and as he opened the door, there was a blast of warm air and a lovely smell of something cooking for supper.

'Is that you, Rhys?' called his mother. 'Come into the kitchen, kettle's on and dinner will be up straight away.'

Rhys made for the stairs intent on getting some dry clothes, 'Be down in a minute. I'm soaked through and starving.' He heard voices, and he heard Nan say, 'That's what his father always said, as soon as he got in the door. I'm starving.' So, thought Rhys, the grandparents were here. Not usually on a Tuesday, and rarely in the evenings. Something must be up. He had a quick bath that immediately warmed him up, got dressed in his favourite jeans and tee-shirt, then made his way to the kitchen.

Immediately, he saw Granddad's unsmiling face, he knew there was trouble of some sort. Rhys pretended he hadn't noticed and cheerfully, called out, 'Hi, my favourite grand-parents, don't usually see you in the week. Something special up?'

Nan looked almost as solemn as granddad, and she looked first at granddad, then his father.

'Who's going to tell him, then?' asked mother.

Granddad turned to his wife, 'You tell him, Mrs, 'cos if I get started I might ...' he paused, 'Well, I don't know what. I'm that cross, I could take my walking stick to him.' Rhys was flabbergasted, he couldn't believe his ears. What on earth have I done to upset him so much, he thought.

Nan was sitting down looking at her hands, then she clasped them together and looked up at Rhys.

'Today, Rhys,' she began. 'Today is Tuesday, our pension day.'

Realisation came immediately to Rhys. Surely not? The old

boy couldn't have believed his little joke. Nan raised her eyebrows and shook her head, his father hid behind the newspaper and his mother stared at him with her hands on her hips, a sure sign she had something to add to the situation.

Rhys crossed the room and stood beside his grandfather, who glared at him.

'So, Rhys,' Nan continued, 'Your granddad, queued up for the pensions, like he said he would but he was such a long time. I'd been to the baker's and the butchers and waited on the corner in all that rain. I got a good soaking, I can tell you. Just waiting for him so we could go home together, especially as my bags were heavy and he always carries them for me.'

'Please don't tell me you believed that little tale I told you. It was a ...'

'Let me finish, Rhys,' Nan said. She took a deep breath, then, 'So I decided to go and look for him. When I reached the post office, there was thousands of people in the queue.'

'Now, mother,' admonished his father, 'surely no more than ten, there's never that many people living in the village.' Nan sniffed,

'There was a long queue and I as walked along it, I could hear people, the men mostly, muttering things like, 'That will be a first", "His said his grandson said it was true" and 'Too good to be true" someone said.' She took her hankie out of her sleeve and wiped her eyes. Rhys wondered for a moment if they might be tears of hidden laughter, but she went on, 'There were three men around your granddad at the counter, all raising their voices,' she pointed at granddad, 'the loudest was his of course. All of them demanding, yes demanding, Rhys, can you believe, a can of lager!'

There was a spluttering behind father's newspaper, mother turned to the cooker to hide her face, and granddad looked both ashamed and embarrassed.

'That's what you said, our lad. You said you read it in the

newspaper,' granddad muttered, and sadly shook his head. 'I believed you, didn't for one moment doubt you.'

'Yes, you did, you silly old fool,' said Nan. 'I remember you said something like it sounded "fishy". You was just living in hopes it was true. Go on, admit it.'

He gave a couple of slow nods. 'Made a right bloody fool of meself, I suppose. As usual, you're right.'

'I'll thank you not to swear in front of the lad.'

'You told me he was not eleven, just a few days ago, he's all grown up according to you.'

Nan tutted. 'Trust you to try to turn the tables.'

Granddad raised his hand and beckoned to Rhys 'Come a bit closer lad.'

'Sorry, Granddad, it was only a joke, I thought you knew that. I'd never ...' before he could say anything else, Granddad's hand swiftly whacked his bottom. Rhys was astonished by this, and the slap really stung.

Rubbing his backside, and ruefully smiling, he said, 'I suppose I deserve that, but it really hurts, Granddad.'

'And that, my lad, is my joke, on you!' grinned Granddad. Then added, 'I did warn you, didn't I? Told you to watch out.'

There was a quiet air of excitement about the village people. It wasn't often that a fair, with a small circus, came anywhere near the village, but this year Fillip's Spring Funfair had been set up in a field some three miles away and would be opening on Saturday. There were smiles as people greeted each other and always with the question, 'Are you going?' No need to ask where. There were nods, and 'Yes,' all round.

Giddy was bursting with anticipation, determined to go. 'We'll go on every ride, especially the bumper cars, and that one that swings right up in the air. We'll find a couple of girls, take them in the ...' here he rolled his eyes and said, dramatically, 'Tunnel of Love. And there'll be candy floss and hot dogs and ...'

'I'm not eating hot dogs before meeting up with girls,' retorted Rhys, 'Could make your breath smell pretty awful, especially the onions. Then what, no ... well you know, carrying-ons, as my nan would say.'

'Got a point there, mate. I suppose we could leave the onions out?'

'Please yourself, but won't taste half as good.' They continued to discuss the merits of each ride, and decided to try as many as possible until funds ran out and arranged to meet around half past seven on Saturday. As they parted, Rhys added, 'And don't expect me to wear one of those, "Kiss me, quick" hats.'

'Spoilsport,' jeered Giddy.

Giddy was late picking Rhys up on Saturday evening and already it was dusk. Rhys saw at once, that his friend was not in good spirits. He was not his bubbly, excitable self and Rhys guessed he'd probably had a row with either his mother or sister.

'What's up with you then?' he enquired.

'Nothing much, got a bit of a headache that a beer will cure. Come on, let's go.' It wasn't long before they could see the bright, flashing lights of the fair then the music once they had parked the bike near the entrance Dumping their helmets on the seats they made their way into the crowds and began to explore. There were stalls selling all sorts of goodies and foods, there were slot machines and roll a coin onto a square promising a win. But their main interest was the rides on offer, some looking more dangerous than others. Again Rhys was surprised that Giddy wasn't rushing from one ride to other, determined to try them all. However, his mood changed when they reached a stall with a notice inviting them to try and shoot the moving ducks.

'No thanks,' said Giddy. 'I'm sure to win one of those pink teddies, and I don't intend to cart one of those around all night.' He was surprised when someone spoke and he turned quickly. There were two girls grinning at him.

'I said,' one of them began, 'I said, I would love a pink teddy. If you win I will give it a good home.' It was like a miracle cure, Rhys saw Giddy perk up at once, the Giddy he knew, all chirpy and flirting.

Giddy grinned and paid for a rifle. 'In that case, I'll have a go.' He examined the rifle carefully, then turned to the stallholder, 'This gun's got a skewwhiff barrel. Look, couldn't hit a bus with it.' The man shrugged his shoulders, didn't say a word, but changed it without making a fuss. Needless to say, only three ducks out of ten fell and there was no teddy bear for his new-found friends. 'Tell you what,' he offered, 'Why don't we treat you girls to a ride or two.' Rhys nodded in agreement, he quite liked the younger of the girls.

'That would be lovely,' answered the elder. 'I'm Pamela and this is Linda.' Skillfully, the boys separated the two girls, Giddy seemed happy with Pamela and Rhys was more than glad to be with Linda.

The four made their way first to the dodgem cars.

'Can't go to a fairground and not try out the dodgems, can we?' joked Giddy.

As the cars were manoeuvred around by the boys who, naturally, deliberately crashed into each other as often as possible, the girls laughed and clung onto their respective partners.

After some serious crashing into each other with a satisfying clunk, a somewhat nervous Linda said, 'You're going to break my neck. Please stop bumping them so often.'

'Not likely,' Rhys retorted, 'That's why they're called bumper cars, designed to bump into the others so as to give them a fright or two. Hang on.' Rhys deftly backed Giddy into a corner, who, by twisting the steering wheel fast, got the car moving backwards and quickly got them back into the fray, and began to retaliate.

'Crikey, I never thought we'd get out of that,' exclaimed Pamela as he once again, collided with Rhys's vehicle.

They ignored the vendor who tried to entice them to ring the bell on top of a tall pole, both knowing they might fail and look foolish in the eyes of their new found friends. They all climbed the steps to the top of the helter-skelter, the boys descended first on their bristly coconut mats and waited for the girls to descend. They were delighted when the girls came into view, their legs were uncovered to just about their knees and both were desperately hanging onto their skirts to prevent any more exposure.

It was as they were walking towards the ghost train ride, that Rhys saw, first the familiar head of wavy, tumbling chestnut hair, then the petite form of Helen. Determined to speak to her, he said to the others, 'You go ahead, I'll catch you up,' and strode away from them.

'Wait up, I'm coming with you,' and Linda hurried after him.

Helen was with a couple of girls, all laughing and

chattering amongst themselves when Rhys caught up with them. He smiled as he said, 'Hello, Helen. I'm ...'

'I know who you are,' she retorted.

'I ...' he began.

'Clear off, pervert,' she snarled. Rhys, a little hurt by this began to leave, but cheered up when he heard one of her exasperated friends say, 'Whatever are you thinking about Ellie? He's bloody gorgeous.'

Rhys looked back at the group and saw Helen shrug. He didn't hear the girl go on to say, 'Not all blokes are perverts. You shouldn't say that.'

'If you worked with the morons I have to suffer and hear their crude remarks, you'd have very little nice to say about any of them,' was the reply.

'Well, you should give this guy a chance, he looked all right to me.'

'If you say so,' sighed Helen.

Rhys and his friends paid and took their places on the ghost train, he with Linda in the first carriage. He was a little surprised when she slid as far away as possible from him, but he edged along the few inches that separated them and reached out to put his arm around her, hoping she would snuggle up. He felt her stiffen and draw herself away. He couldn't understand, and wasn't sure what to think, so shifted himself away so as not to frighten or offend her.

They were the first to reach the end of the ride, and Rhys was not surprised to see Giddy and Pamela in a serious clinch as they emerged from the tunnel. Giddy waved, and shouted, 'We're going round again!'

As he laughed he looked at Linda who was obviously sulking and scuffing her feet. 'What's up with you?' he asked as he took her hand. Snatching her hand away, she replied, 'You didn't kiss me, or even try.'

'Hold on a minute, I tried to, but, but you made damn sure I, I didn't,' he stammered.

'Well, I couldn't be sure could I? Not when that girl called you a pervert.' Rhys shook his head,

'She says that to all the lads. None of us take any notice. I think she's afraid of men, that's all.' It wasn't quite true, he really had no idea why Helen called him a pervert, but he felt he ought to reassure Linda. 'Tell you what, you want to kiss? Let's find somewhere quiet then, so I can make it up to you.' She beamed up at him and he took her hand and together they threaded their way through the crowd towards the line of caravans fringing the fair. The far side of the caravans were in darkness and the sounds of the fair seemed faded. 'This should be alright,' Rhys said as he took her in his arms and kissed her, gently at first. Her response was more than he expected, almost demanding something more.

'Hmm,' he murmured, 'You like that? Up to expectations?'

She nodded and snuggled further into his arms.

As he kissed her again with the same response, he pondered over what to do next. Should he risk going a bit further or was she just teasing? He'd been teased before and knew girls' techniques of leading a fellow on, then dropping him at the last minute. Should he, or wait to see what happens he thought, as he kissed her again. Yes, he told himself, I'll take a chance. Slowly he slid his hand up towards her chest, and almost succeeded when a shrill voice yelled at him, 'What do you think you're doing to my sister?' She's only fifteen.'

Her call was immediately followed by a weak, breathless Giddy asking, 'Take me home, Rhys, I'm feeling rotten.'

Rhys's mind was to-ing and fro-in between these two statements. He looked first at Linda, and was shocked to see that her looks defied her age. If he had gone any further he realised he could have been in a lot of trouble. He turned to Giddy and saw his friend's white face with rivulets of perspiration running down his cheeks. Everything went out of his mind. His friend came first. Swiftly, he put his arm around Giddy's waist, and softly said, 'Come on, sunshine, let's go,' and left the now bickering girls.

As Giddy struggled to get on the pillion seat, Rhys ordered, 'Put your helmet on.'

'Shut up. Just get me home,' moaned Giddy. Rhys carefully rode the bike towards home and was surprised when Giddy put his arms around his waist and clung on tightly. A few moments later Rhys was alarmed as Giddy slumped onto his back and he felt the heat of his friend's body through his jacket. He was convinced, without a doubt that his best friend was very ill. Without hesitating, he turned the bike around, and headed straight for the hospital. On arrival, he had great difficulty getting Giddy off the bike, 'Hang on there,' he said as parked the bike securely. But Giddy was past hearing, and slid in a heap to the ground. In no time at all, Giddy was taken away by medical staff, and Rhys, thoroughly concerned for his friend's welfare, was close to tears as he made his way home.

When Rhys finally reached home around midnight, and before his mother could scold him about the lateness of his return, he said, 'Giddy's in hospital.'

'You haven't had an accident, have you?' There was anxiety in his father's voice. 'Tell me you haven't. I've warned the pair of you time and time again.'

Before Rhys could answer, his mother, full of concern, asked, 'But you're alright love?'

'Giddy is ill so I took him to the hospital.' As he slowly began to climb the stairs to his room, he added, 'I am so tired. I'll tell you about it in the morning.' His parents, seeing their son so upset, said nothing more.

Mid-Sunday morning, Rhys was awakened by the sound of the telephone ringing. His mother answered it, and he heard her say in hushed tones, 'Oh, dear. I'm so sorry to hear that.' He heard the click of the receiver being replaced, then a muffled conversation between his parents, and he suspected the worst news possible. It wasn't long before he heard footsteps on the stairs and promptly pulled the bedclothes over his head. He was convinced his lifelong friend had died, and he didn't want to hear this dreadful news confirmed. There was a soft knock on his door that he ignored. He wriggled further under the covers when someone sat heavily down on the bed and shook his shoulder.

Softly, he heard his mother say, 'Rhys, love, we've just had a call from Giddy's mother, she ...' She stopped when she heard Rhys's muffled voice.

'Go away. I don't want to know.'

'Come out from under there.'

'No, you're only going to tell me something's happened to Giddy. That he's, that he's ...'

'No, no. It's not bad news.' She sighed, knowing her next few words might be equally upsetting for him. 'Come out now, and listen to me.'

Reluctantly he drew the covers away from his face, clutching them fiercely so as to return to his little haven should the news be awful.

When he finally emerged, she was dismayed to see his stricken face, awash with tears. 'Rhys, love,' she whispered, as she reached out her arms to him. He leaned against her, with his head on her shoulder, and she stroked his hair. 'Rhys love, Giddy has meningitis; he is very poorly.' She hesitated before adding, 'But, love, he is in a coma, he's in a deep sleep, that should help him get better quickly.'

She heard Rhys mumble something, and asked, 'What did you say?'

Lifting his head and looking up at her, he answered, 'For how long?'

'No one knows for how long, it's just nature's way of healing.'

'If it's too long he'll starve, won't he? I mean, how can he eat if he's asleep?' She felt his body begin to shake, then heard him choke out, 'He's going to die, I know it.'

'Rhys, the doctors say because he has been vaccinated and he is young and a fighter, the chances of him recovering are fairly good.' Rhys eased himself out of her arms and sat up. 'Also, they said, that the antibiotics they are giving him, will be a great help. Now, that's better news than you thought, isn't it?' She felt him squirm a little and tried to soothe him.

'But that means ... You said his chances are fairly good, so that's not the same as saying they are very good, is it? He could die couldn't he? That wouldn't be fair, would it? He's my best friend. He's not done anything bad, he doesn't deserve to die.'

Sobs began to surface, and his mother full of concern, took his hand said, 'No one has said anything about dying, Rhys.

Yes, he needs extra special care, that's why he's in the Intensive Care Unit, so they can do their best for him. It's going to take a long time, and there could be some complications, but everyone is hopeful, and you must be too.' She let go of him, and stood up. 'Now, get up, have a wash and perhaps you could pop round and see Mrs Cooper, give her a hand maybe, she'd like that.' She sighed, 'Poor woman, she is beside herself with worry. She and Mr Cooper ought to be at the hospital together, but someone has to look after the young ones.' Kissing the top of his head, she added, 'Perhaps you can think of something to help out. Come on now, move.'

It was just after eleven o'clock when Rhys knocked on the Cooper's door and Mrs Cooper opened it. Rhys saw at once by her white face, how upset she was. 'Come on in for a bit,' she said, and stood back to let him enter. As she stepped inside, she grabbed his hand and said, 'Oh, Rhys, thank you, thank you for looking after Giddy for us. He could have died you know, if you hadn't been so quick to see how poorly he was.'

Rhys blushed, and looked at his feet and mumbled, 'He would have done the same for me, Mrs Cooper, we've been mates for a long time, and he he ...' He almost choked on a sudden sob rising, 'he was ...'

Mrs Cooper patted his arm, 'It's okay, lad. I understand, things like that shouldn't happen to young folk to cope with. It's all so, so sudden to take in.' She slowly led the way to the kitchen where Giddy's brothers and sisters were seated around the table. Rhys knew there were two girls, and two boys. Mary Jane, who was fifteen, two years younger than Giddy and Nancy who was twelve. Next came ten-year-old William and lastly there was the youngest, Dylan who was nearly seven. Usually there was uproar in the kitchen, the children would be shouting, laughing, teasing and, especially the boys, tumbling about. Today, they were a solemn group, quietly trying to do their school homework.

'I thought, well my mam said, perhaps I could help out in

some way, Mrs Cooper, so that you and Mr Cooper could visit G... er,' Rhys hesitated, then quickly went on, 'Idris together. He would like that, seeing you together.'

'Well, that's very thoughtful of you both, but I think we can manage.'

'Mam,' interrupted Mary Jane, who secretly thought Rhys was the best boy she ever knew, 'Rhys is very good at math and William is so behind, I've got my own homework to do, perhaps Rhys could help him a bit?'

'What do you think, Rhys, can you sort William out for us?'

Rhys had always hated having to do homework and had breathed a sigh of relief when, at the end of the final school year, he had no longer had to submit his efforts. Of course, homework from college was a different matter, his future, as his father kept reminding him, depended on good results.

'Yes, no problem,' he answered and walked over to the table, elbowing his way beside William as he said, 'Move over. Let me see.' All settled down quietly to work, Rhys suspected that, like himself, they were all longing to hear some good news about Giddy. At one o'clock, Mrs Cooper invited Rhys to stay for some dinner, 'Just something quick today, as we want to be at the hospital dead on two,' she explained.

Rhys declined politely, 'Thank you, Mrs Cooper, but Mam is expecting me home.'

Mary Jane was quick to ask, 'Will you come again tomorrow, Rhys? After work, we will all have lots more homework, and you have been so good with William.'

'Of course, I was intending to do so, to find out when Giddy might be coming home.'

Mrs Cooper put her hand on his shoulder, as she softly said, 'We don't think that will be for some time yet, Rhys. The doctors are doing their best and are very hopeful. We'll let you know, but, as I say, it could be a few days, even a week or two before we can be sure he is out of the woods.'

What could he say? 'I hope it will be sooner than that, he

owes me one pound an' twenty-three p's.' This made her smile and the children laugh. As cheerfully as he could muster, he said 'See you all tomorrow. I'll be here around half-six after my dinner.'

True to his word, Rhys arrived at the Cooper's house on time. The kitchen was in an uproar. Mrs Cooper was trying to bite into a sandwich as she was putting her coat on and issuing out orders left, right and centre. Rhys took in the situation and immediately helped her shrug into her coat. 'Thank you, Rhys. I've got to get the bus this evening, Mr Cooper is working late, but he's going to get to the hospital later, and bring me home.'

The bus thought Rhys. Really the lifeline of villagers without their own means of transport, always on time every day at thirty-nine minutes past the hour. It was already six twenty-five.

Mrs Cooper sighed. Then looking at her family she began again. 'Mary Jane, you're in charge of clearing up, do the dishes and tidy everywhere.' Rhys saw Mary Jane scowl.

'And you Nancy, will help her, understand? Dry the dishes and set the table for breakfast.'

It was a very indignant Nancy who with a raised voice said, 'Wipe up? I want to wash up,' and promptly stomped across the room.

'Do as you're told, for once,' snapped back her mother.

'Giddy, wouldn't do it. He'd say no, and clear off.'

Mrs Cooper glowered at her, 'Yes, and I'd box his ears for his cheek.' She turned to Rhys and pointed at him, 'And you, you can take the bins out for the bin men tomorrow, then check on William and that Miss ...' she pointed to Nancy, 'to see if they have finished their homework.' She glanced around the kitchen, then at her children and tried to smile at them to reassure them. 'Now then, smiles all round please and a big hello for your poorly brother.'

There was a murmuring amongst them saying things like, 'Get well,' and 'miss you.'

'I'm off now,' she said, as she bent to pick up the rest of her sandwich to eat on the way.

Everyone gave a quiet chuckle as the cheese in her sandwich slid out and fell to the floor. For a few moments, she stood as if fixed and stared at it, then burst into tears.

Mary Jane rushed across and put her arms around her mother, and Rhys pulled up a chair and told her to sit down for a moment. Within seconds Mrs Cooper jumped up in alarm, 'The bus,' she cried, 'I'll miss the bus.'

A sudden idea came to Rhys. 'Sit down, Mrs C. I'll sort it. Mary, make your mam another sandwich,' he commanded and left the room.

'Where's he gone?' asked Dylan.

William went to the door and came back saying, 'He's on the phone.' Everyone was quiet hoping to hear what Rhys was saying, but the conversation was ending, 'Right, see you soon, then. Bye.' He was beaming as he came back to the family, 'That's sorted then,' he told them. 'Someone's going to give you a lift to the hospital, and you'll be there long before the bus, Mrs C.'

It wasn't long before there was a knock on the door and Dylan, full of curiosity, rushed to let in the mystery caller.

'Now then, Mrs Cooper, let's be on our way,' said Emlyn. 'Don't you ever get the bus again, just call me. I'll be glad to take you. Especially if it helps to get that lad of yours better.' On the way out, Mrs Cooper called back over her shoulder, 'Rhys, love make sure Dylan cleans his teeth before he gets into bed.'

As Emlyn helped Mrs Cooper into the car, he turned to Rhys and smiled as he said, 'Told Megan where I was going, told her how you're helping out the family, and guess what she said?'

'Something sarcastic I expect, I'm still in her bad books.'

Emlyn laughed as he got into the car and settled on his seat. 'Well, you certainly asked for it, didn't you? All that mess you left.'

Rhys had a pang of guilt, he never did go back to help her tidy the kitchen. He shrugged his shoulders, 'Well, what did she say then?'

'She said, and I'm not sure I agree with her mind, she said, "Our Rhys! Bless him, a real hero. I knew he was a good lad. Tell him, I'll have some Welsh cakes ready when he comes over next." There now, that's not sarcastic is it? Seems you're off the hook. Bye now, and get back to your duties.'

When Rhys returned to the kitchen, the siblings were bickering and at first he was at a loss as to what to do. He smiled to himself as inspiration came to him – he would do an Emlyn on them. Standing in the middle of the kitchen, hands on hips he bellowed, 'Enough!' The result was the same as in Emlyn's household. Everyone stopped, the Cooper children almost stunned, were silent, not knowing what to expect. Emlyn's family, of course, knew at once that they were in trouble.

'That's better,' Rhys began, 'We've all got jobs to do to help your mother. So … it looks like you've all finished your supper now take your plates and mugs to the sink ready for Mary Jane.'

There were a few grumbles as they did as he said, but William shouted, 'Hurray,' when Rhys reminded them that he had the stinky job of sorting out the dustbins. Ten minutes later, all were seated at the table doing homework.

Without giving answers, Rhys guided William through his math work. 'You're as smart as Giddy in math,' he told Rhys.

'That's because we learned the secret of numbers in school.'

'A secret?'

'Well, not really a secret, anyone who wants to get better at sums use these.'

William, not sure if Rhys was joking, 'I suppose you wouldn't tell me, would you?'

'I'll think about it.' William plodded on with the work, sighing as the answers were rejected by his helper and he had to start again.

'Who told you, anyway?' he mumbled.

'At the time, if I had listened properly, the teacher, but it was Giddy's girlfriend who showed him, and he told me.' Four pairs of eyes stared at him in amazement. Giddy had a girlfriend and they didn't know. At once Rhys saw he had probably caused a problem for his friend when he came home. His heart lightened, for the first time in two days, he had thought positively about Giddy getting better.

'What's her name?' Mary Jane asked.

'Not going to tell you that. I know you lot, you'll be teasing Giddy, and besides it was a very long time ago.' More questions were fired at him straight away, but he shrugged them all off, saying that Giddy would tell them if he wanted to in good time.

William sidled up to Rhys, and whispered, 'Will you tell me, the secret please, Rhys. I want to be as good as Giddy, and he's really, really clever.'

'I will, but it means hard work to start with, then everything will become much easier.'

'I'll try, I will, I promise.'

Just learn your times table by heart, that's all there is to it. Learn every one of them so that when someone says eight times eight for example, your brain will quickly tell you the answer, really quickly 'cos it's there in your memory.'

It was time for Dylan to get ready for bed. Rhys anticipated some resistance from the boy, but this was something he had dealt with when getting his niece and nephew upstairs to bed.

'Bedtime, Dylan. Let's get up them stairs.'

There was the universal cry of, 'Do I have to?'

'Yes, say goodnight and show me your room.'

Dragging his feet, and obviously tired and ready for bed, he muttered, 'Night, night,' and followed Rhys.

Brushing of teeth was no problem, but Dylan was defiant when told to wash his face. After a short stand-off, Dylan said, 'Only if you tell me a story.' Rhys didn't think he'd escaped that chore anyway, and agreed. As they entered the untidy bedroom, Rhys saw there were bunk beds and a single.

'I sleep on the top bunk and William is underneath me. He snores and that's Giddy's bed.' Pointing to the single one. He beamed up at Rhys, 'And he said I could have it when he joined the army.'

The army, Rhys was amazed at this news. Surely not Rhys thought to himself. When was that decided? Never said anything to me about joining the army. No, he convinced himself, I hope he's only teasing the boy. There's no way I'm going into the army with him, and that's final.

Pyjamas on and tucked up in bed, Rhys asked him what story would he like.

'The one Giddy always tells me. That book over there.'

Rhys crossed the room and picked up the book on the table beside Giddy's bed, and read, *The Tropic of Ruislip*. Giddy had been telling him about it a couple of weeks ago. A book with a variety of sexual dreams, and scandals.

'Are you sure, he reads this to you? It's a grown-up's story.'

'Yes, of course he does, I said so, didn't I?'

At a loss as to what to do, Rhys asked, 'So tell me what's it about.'

Dylan laughed, Rhys was unnerved. What was the boy going to say?

Snuggling down under the covers, he said, 'I don't know. I just like to hear Giddy's voice, and before you know it, I'm asleep. Never hear very much. I get too tired to listen properly.'

Rhys gave a huge sigh of relief. 'Well, I'll sort out something different for tonight. How about this?' and he picked up a copy of *The B.F.G.*

'Yes please, that's my favourite.'

Rhys began to read but four pages in, and Dylan was asleep. Gently, Rhys lifted the child into his own bed.

It was just after nine o'clock when Rhys, convinced he was more tired than he had ever been, sat down and leaned back on the sofa. Everywhere was tidy and William was reading in Giddy's bed, assuring Rhys that he was allowed to sleep there if he wanted. Mary Jane came and sat down beside him, equally exhausted. She was far too close to him, their thighs almost touching and he wriggled away from her. 'Have you got a girlfriend?' she asked.

How could he answer? He dearly would like to say 'yes' but at present there seemed little hope of Helen taking on that role. He didn't want to say, 'No,' because he intended that one day, she would be his girlfriend.

He answered, 'Sort of,' and hoped that would satisfy Mary Jane.

'So,' she tilted her head as she looked at him, 'does that mean you haven't at present?'

'At present, I'm sitting here with you, absolutely shattered.' He could see she was pleased with his answer and he realized she thought it meant more than he had intended. 'How about you making us a drink? I'd like a chocolate one if you've got any, otherwise, a tea will do.'

She jumped up immediately, 'Of course, I'll make you a drink. I think there is some cocoa or something chocolaty in the kitchen,' she replied. He could tell she was happy to be able to do something for him.

Quickly, he moved into a single armchair and picked up a stray newspaper. When she returned with two mugs, she was surprised and said, 'Oh, I thought we could be together on the sofa, it was so cosy.' Luckily, before he could say anything, the door opened and Mr and Mrs Cooper came in.

Rhys immediately stood up, and asked, 'Any news? Please say he is awake.'

'No lad,' Mr Cooper replied. 'Still out for the count. I can only say to you what the doctor told us, "It could be some time yet before we see any improvement".'

In bed that night, Rhys pondered over the evening events. Although he was perfectly happy in his own home, he thought that, somehow, he was missing out not having a noisy, busy, laughing, bickering family. Giddy was never far from his thoughts and he wondered, like he did in his childhood when his brother was missing, should he wish upon a star. That worked out, then told himself not to be so daft. Then there was the question of his friend joining the army. Rhys thought he'd have too as well, just to keep his friend out of trouble. But, would they be together, he wondered. I'll ask Emlyn, he'll know. Briefly, his thoughts turned to Helen but he quickly dismissed them. She'd made it quite clear she wasn't interested, and so be it, he told himself. Forget her. As he settled down to sleep he told himself, anyway, who knows – tomorrow Giddy may well wake up.

True to his word, Rhys visited the Cooper household in the evenings. Mrs Cooper was always glad to see him and gave him a warm welcome, making sure there was a snack for him to enjoy once the younger children were in bed. William settled down quickly to his homework under Rhys's supervision, and never argued as always happened every night with Giddy, according to Mary Jane. Nancy rarely asked for help, and was still resisting to do any household duties, putting on an act of defiance or sulking, but in the end, with some bribes, usually a later bedtime, or Rhys's cajoling her, the chores got done.

Being alone with Mary Jane, which wasn't very often, made Rhys wary. She was quite an attractive fifteen-year-old girl he conceded, but was his best friend's sister. This would certainly cause friction between them as Giddy was well aware of Rhys's, and his own, intentions towards girls. Another thing, fifteen! He was still horrified at being caught by the sister of his latest encounter not so many days ago. Thankfully, Mary Jane seemed to sense his still friendly but cool manner and she made no further advances for his attention.

When the parents returned on Wednesday evening, the news was the same as Monday's and Tuesday's, that there was no change in Giddy yet, and Rhys, like the previous nights, was despondent as he walked home.

Thursday, College day. A break from site work. He knew it was his own fault when, more than once during the week, Mr Bert had reasons to be sharp with him. He was asked to make a mug of builders' brew, strong tea. He took it across to Mr Bert, who, without looking, stretched out his hand, took the mug and with a sigh of content, lifted it to his lips and took a large swallow. Rhys was astounded when the tea was spluttered all over both of them. What was wrong, he asked himself? Mr Bert told him in no uncertain terms, adding a few swear words. Rhys had forgotten to boil the kettle, and so cold water had been poured over a teabag. It wasn't long before a mug of fresh hot tea was handed to Mr Bert by an embarrassed apprentice. Rhys was relieved to see him laughing with the rest of the men when he told of the incident.

Another day, the crew had chosen the fillings for their sandwiches and rolls, gave Rhys the money and sent him off to buy them from the local baker's shop. On his way, his mind drifted off and he began a list of 'what ifs'. What if Giddy died? What if his mind was so damaged and he was unable to remember anything at all? What if he couldn't play rugby again? What if? What if? The negative thoughts were endless. It was no surprise to him when in the baker's, that he could hardly remember who had wanted what. Some he remembered from past visits, but took a guess at others. On his return, needless to say, there was a bit of grumbling, someone swore and he ducked a clip around the head from an electrician who had wanted chicken and got corn beef.

Yesterday afternoon, Wednesday, he had been asked to saw off some noggins, a strut that was fixed between ceiling joists to add strength. There was a five mm shortfall of the measurements he was given. Mr Bert had come down the ladder fast and had grabbed him on the shoulders. With his face close to Rhys's he demanded, 'What the hell is wrong with you, boy? Yer can't be making mistakes like that. Weren't you listening? Ask, if you're not sure, for God's sake.'

Rhys could only answer, 'Sorry.'

'Sorry isn't good enough.' He dropped his hands to sides and looked at the young lad's face, seeing his distress. 'What's up with you, lad?' he asked gently. 'What's troubling you?' After hearing from Rhys the reasons, he patted him on the shoulder. 'You can only hope for the best, he's in good hands. My boy was in that hospital, and he pulled through.' As he began to climb back up the ladder, he added, 'Keep your mind on your work, remember everyone one of us here is dependent on the other. Your friend will be ok, now let's have some noggins for me to get on, dead on the measurements I gave you.'

Mr Bert was right, Rhys knew he had to concentrate if he was to get City and Guilds recognition at the end of his indenture. As it happened, the morning was spent mainly on calculations, and these had occupied his mind fully so he was surprised when it was lunchtime. In the canteen he ordered his egg and chips and enjoyed the usual banter from the other students. It was when he was alone walking towards the work studio, thoughts of Giddy sneaked back into his mind. Miserably making his way along the corridor, head down and hands in pocket, he was suddenly stopped in his tracks. Looking up he saw Helen smiling at him.

'Hi Rhys,' she began, 'I just want to say sorry about last ...'

Rhys shrugged and mumbled, 'That's alright. Forget it,' and edged his way around her.

'Oh,' she said, surprised at his short answer. Then, 'Suit yourself,' and quickly left him.

Rhys swore to himself, knowing he had truly missed the opportunity he had been angling for over the last few months. He turned to try to put matters right, but she had gone. Ruefully, he blamed Giddy, just wait 'til he was home, I'm going to give him a hard time, he told himself.

In the evening he made his way to the Cooper's house, and the evening was spent like the past three. Everything changed when Mr and Mrs Cooper came home. Mr Cooper was smiling and Mrs Cooper, her eyes awash with tears, was beaming. Mary Jane and Rhys looked at them, then at each other, both of them full of hope. 'Mam, is it ... is it good news? Is our Giddy better?' asked Mary Jane. Rhys held his breath waiting for the answer.

Mr Cooper sat down heavily in his armchair and stretched

out. 'Aye,' he said, 'but best if your mam told you.'

Mrs Cooper was indeed bursting with news. 'Well,' she began. 'It's like this. I was sitting beside the poor lad, all those tubes and things in his arm and more up his nose, and I was holding his hand and willing him to wake up like I do every evening. Mr Cooper was a bit behind me as he had to park the car but I couldn't wait to see my boy.' She was interrupted.

'They charge a fortune to park. Didn't ought to be allowed for visitors seeing their sick folk.'

Mary Jane glared at him but spoke quietly to her mother. 'Go on Mam, please.'

'Your dad stopped at the little café in the foyer to get us both a cup of tea, and when he entered the room, the big soft ape, he yelled ...'

'No I didn't.'

'Yes you did, you shouted at him.' She turned to the listeners and nodded. 'He shouted, "You lazy little blighter. Get up now. No more of this nonsense."' Her eyes filled up again and she sniffed. 'And, and ... would you believe, I swear I saw one of Giddy's eyelids slowly, oh very, very slowly open, then close down again.' She was laughing now, 'See, he's beginning to come round at last,' and she looked at Mr Cooper who nodded.

'Didn't see it meself, but your mam was sure. So I went over and ...'

'And he said, "What you playing at son. Frightening your mother to death you are" and we both saw ... both of us didn't we?'

We saw the lad's eyes open.' There was a pause, 'then they shut down again so fast, well you wouldn't believe it had happened if you hadn't been there.'

Mrs Cooper clasped hands together, lifted her shoulders and smiled, He could be home soon, and I'll look after him myself. No place like home to get better.'

'Now don't get over-excited, mother,' Mr Cooper warned.

'Remember, the doctor said this sometimes happen. We got to wait a while longer to be sure.'

'Oh, I'm certain sure,' she replied. 'Now Rhys you pop off home and tell your folks the good news and Mary love, get us a cup of tea and some biscuits to celebrate.'

'Prefer a beer meself,' Mr Cooper whispered to Rhys.

There was a jauntiness in Rhys's walk as he made his way home that night.

Ten minutes was all Rhys was allowed on his first visit to the hospital. Giddy was now off the danger list, and considered to be stable, or as it had been explained to him, he was not likely to get worse. Although he had been told again and again by Giddy's parents, he was hardly able to hide his shock despite their warnings when he saw his friend. As he approached the bed, Giddy slightly raised his arm in greeting. Rhys smiled and raised his hand in return, hoping Giddy would not see how upset he was. Look at him, Rhys thought, his arm is stick thin and I can see the knobby bones of his elbow and fingers. Arriving at the bedside and drawing up a chair, he softly asked, 'How you doing mate?'

Through pale lips, Giddy gave a weak smile, then nodded and in a hoarse whisper answered, 'Better for seeing you.' He took a breath, before adding, 'Too many fussing me,' then closed his eyes for a few moments.

Rhys noticed how white his face was, and the usual sparkling, mischievous blue eyes, were dull and almost covered by his drooping eyelids. Hoping to cheer his friend up, he said, 'You need a haircut and it's time you started shaving.' There was no quip in return, just another weak smile and Rhys saw that his friend was almost asleep. 'I'll come again at the weekend, I promise,' he said as he replaced the chair, then pulled on his jacket. 'We'll catch up on Saturday, bye for now, mate.'

It was a week before Rhys saw his friend again, it was decided that the Coopers would visit Giddy on Saturday evening, and Rhys could spend an hour with him in the afternoon. As soon as he entered the ward, Rhys's face lit up. From the entrance he could see Giddy was much stronger. 'Wow! Look at you,' he said when he reached the bedside. 'What's perked you up, then?'

There was a wide grin on Giddy's face as he said, 'Am I glad to see you. Lot of fogies in here. Got no idea what's it like to by young.' He nodded to an elderly patient across the room. 'That ol' codger snores all night and moans all day.'

'A bit like you then. What you doing in bed? Your folks told me you can sit in a chair.'

'They like everyone in bed for visiting time, makes the ward look tidy, I'm told.' He leaned across and poked Rhys in the ribs, 'And don't you go round saying things like that, I'd rather be dead.'

Rhys gasped. 'You nearly was, you idiot. Frightened me and everyone else. Don't say things like that.'

Seeing his friend was upset, Giddy was immediately ashamed of himself. 'Sorry, Rhys, you know what I meant,' he said softly. When he got a gentle punch on his arm, he smiled. 'You know what,' he hesitated, 'What I want to say is ...'

Rhys could see he was almost in tears.

'What are you trying to say, for goodness' sake. Cheer up. You're not dead after all, are you?'

'That's just it. You saved my life and, well, I owe you.'

Rhys laughed as he retorted, 'I must have been mad,' and together they laughed. Pulling on his jacket, Rhys stood up. 'Come on, give us a smile. You'll be out of here before you know it, then we'll make some plans.'

On Rhys's next visit a few days later, he was surprised at the change in his friend. Beaming with delight, as he reached Giddy's bed, he threw some magazines on the bed and said, 'You old fraud. You look much better than the last time I was here. Your mam told me you were getting along nicely, but I didn't expect to see you as good as this.'

'Yes, I am feeling a lot better, thanks.' Giddy replied as he picked up the magazines, turned them over, then said, 'Well, I appreciate the magazines, two motorbike ones and a comic. Thanks, mate, couldn't you reach the top shelf?'

'Behave yourself. Anything like that would give you a

relapse.'

'I don't think so. Look,' he said pointing to a young nurse entering the ward, 'See what I mean? That's one, the only one compensation being in here. Lots and lots of pretty talent, every day.'

'Are you telling me ...'

'Well,' Giddy grinned, 'I keep trying, but they all say the same thing.'

Rhys interrupted him, 'You're too cheeky, or push off, or you're not my type, I bet.'

'None of those,' Giddy sighed, 'They all say I'm too young, not enough experience. I tell them they could give me some experience. They just laugh, then shove a thermometer in my mouth to shut me up.'

Rhys laughed, 'They've got a point. Anyway, here's a couple of motorbike mags. That should keep you interested. You like motorbikes if my memory serves me right. It's so hot in here,' he complained. As he wriggled off his jacket, a buff envelope fell out of the pocket. 'Oh,' he said, 'I nearly forgot. These are for you.'

As Giddy reached out to take the envelope, he saw H.M.S. across the top, and queried, 'What is it? I don't earn enough to pay more tax. They take enough as it is.' He opened the envelope, gasped, and looked at Rhys. 'What the heck is this?' he asked.

'Your application to join the army.'

Giddy's jaw dropped as he squealed, 'What!' He took a deep breath, 'This is one of your jokes isn't it?'

'Would I joke about something like this?'

'But why. What made you think I wanted to join up?'

Rhys was inwardly laughing, but in a serious tone he answered, 'Dylan told me.'

'Dylan!'

'Yep, he told me you said to him that when you went into the army, he could have your bed. Quite serious he was.

What's more, he's sleeping in your bed right now while you're in here.'

'The little ...'

'Oh, don't worry it'll be fun. I'll join up with you.'

'You're kidding.'

'Seriously, I got my papers too. When Dylan said that, I thought, well someone's got to keep you out of trouble. You know what you're like. Anyway, you don't have to make up your mind yet, not 'til you're at least seventeen.'

Giddy slumped back on his pillows. 'Thank goodness for that. There's no way I'm going in the army. Do this, get that, volunteer needed and someone will point at me. No way. And what's more, I'll tan that little brat when I get home.'

The ward doors swung open and a nurse wheeled in the tea trolley rattling with china cups and saucers. 'Just what I could do with,' said Rhys. 'I'm parched.'

'You'll be lucky, patients only in here.'

'Wanna bet?' Giddy grinned knowing his friend had a plan. Sure enough, when the nurse approached to ask Giddy did he want milk and sugar, Rhys butted in quickly. 'My friend says he is very hot and thirsty. Could you let him have two cups? That might help him a bit.'

The unsuspecting nurse, replied, 'Of course, and when I've finished, I'll come back and take your temperature, just to make sure you're all right. Milk and sugar?' Giddy nodded and two cups of tea were set down on the locker. The boys waited a moment or two while she served the person in the next bed, and as soon as she had moved further down the ward took a cup each.

Lifting his cup, smugly Rhys said, 'Told you so. Cheers.'

After a few mouthfuls, Giddy said, 'Did my mam tell you, I might be home soon? Maybe Saturday with luck.'

'That'll be great. Well done, mate.' They were quiet for a few moments, until Rhys suddenly said, 'You could be out before then if you wanted.'

'What do you mean?' Rhys had begun to chuckle softly, 'Listen, remember when I was a kid and you visited me in hospital?'

'Yes, your head was all bandaged up and drips everywhere and gave me a fright.'

'Not as bad as the one you gave me last week.'

'Don't remind me.'

'You remember when I was able to get out of bed, and I hid behind the curtains and ...'

'I told the nurse you was missing and everyone began searching and wasn't that sister cross when she found you back in bed.'

'She told me off rotten when you had gone.'

'Worth it though, wasn't it?' and they began to chuckle. 'But I reckon the best was when you hid and I stuffed the bed with pillows and bashed the life out of them.' Both of them began to laugh.

'And that roly-poly nurse came rushing down the ward, absolutely horrified she was.'

'And one of the kid's visitors rushed across the room thinking to rescue me, but tripped and fell over.' They were laughing now so loudly that everyone in the ward had turned to see what was going on.

'Yes, there was absolute pandemonium and the doctor rushed in and said ...'

'Crikey. Yes, so he did, and he didn't half pinch my ear as he said, he said ...' Giddy's eyes widened and he looked at Rhys as he went on. 'He said, "Get out of here, don't you ever come back. I'll see you get thrown out".'

'Exactly. Tell the doctor next time he comes to see you, it might work!'

'He'd never fall for that. Believe me, I've tried all sorts to get out, but he won't listen.' Then they began laughing again, knowing that there was no way Giddy was going home until everyone was satisfied with his progress.

Within three weeks, Giddy was back at work. It took a little persuading, on his part, to get signed off by his doctor, and a good number of bickering, cajoling and his mother's tears before she very unwillingly, agreed he could return to work, 'but I'll have words with Mr Davies before you start back.'

Giddy sighed before saying, 'Now Mum, don't interfere.'

'No, I won't, but I will say my piece.'

Rolling his eyes, Giddy asked, 'Like what?'

'No heavy lifting and light duties for a start,' she snapped. 'In fact, I'll phone right now.' and promptly made her way to the telephone. Giddy shrugged, he'd soon sorted things out when he met up with Mr Davies the following Monday.

It wasn't long before he was seeking some sort of adventure. After much thought, he knew that what he really wanted was to get away from the constant cautions from his father – 'Are you tired son? Not overdoing it are you? Best have an early night' – and the fussing by his mother as soon as he entered the house. Thankfully, he was able to meet up with Rhys, who, according to Mam, 'Will watch out for you.' It was a June Saturday evening, and they were once again enjoying an illicit beer in the nearby village. 'Got any ideas for next weekend, Rhys? I could do with a break.'

Rhys smiled, 'Oh, yes, my friend.'

Giddy perked up at once as he admitted to himself, that sometimes, not often, but sometimes Rhys had a good idea. 'Like what, for instance?'

'How about we go camping for the weekend. There's a good site and we could go fishing.'

'Fishing! That's for old men.'

'Wait a minute. Do you think your folks will let you go if we said there was a club there?'

Giddy laughed.

'I thought not, but if we say we're going fishing, a nice and safe spot and a quiet rest for you, I reckon that might work.'

'Did you say there is a club? What sort of club?'

'One with food, drinks, music, perhaps a girl or two.' Giddy jumped down from his bar stool and with a broad grin, lightly punched Rhys's arm. 'Brilliant,' and he did a quick twirl, splashing his drink over Rhys.

'Hey, steady on, you idiot. Look what you've done to my tee shirt?'

'Oh, don't make such a fuss.' Giddy gave Rhys another punch. 'You're a genius, know that? A ruddy genius.'

'You like the idea then?'

The answer was a vigorous nodding from his delighted friend.

'Right. Emlyn's got one of those igloo tents, I expect he will lend it to us. I'll come round tomorrow and we will make arrangements. Okay?'

'Hang on a mo, will you?' Giddy said. 'I think it would be better if I came round to yours.'

'Why?'

Taking a deep breath, he replied, 'The family! Once they think we're plotting something, one of them at least, will be earwigging.' Shaking his head, he continued, 'Then the parents will hear about it, and before you know it, my mam will be dreaming up all sorts of horrors that might happen, and to keep the peace, Dad will ban me from going.'

'Never thought of that. Yep, see you around two then, suit you?'

They had decided not to tell the parents until Thursday evening, knowing that any earlier, both would probably be nagged to death. As it was, the first thing Rhys's mother said was, 'No Rhys, the boy's not fit enough and I don't want you being responsible for him. What if ...'

Rhys sighed, here we go, he thought. 'Mam, Giddy's fine. Do you think the doctor would have let him go back to work if he wasn't?'

'That boy is a fool to himself. There'll be trouble, you can bet your life on it. No, Rhys, I think you'd both better wait a while, perhaps in August, he'll be stronger then.'

Dad interrupted, 'Aye, and got a bit more sense by then too.'

'We've made up our minds. Giddy needs to get away for a bit of a break from ...' He was reluctant to say that Mrs Cooper was actually going over the top with mothering his friend. 'Well, from everything. Time to forget his illness, and have some fun.' Rhys smiled, 'He wants an adventure.' Rhys wasn't sure what the reaction would be when he added, 'so we're going fishing. Can't be any harm in that can there?'

Dad laughed, 'I'll bet anything, that you two will get into some sort of mess. Why, lad, you can't even keep quiet for a minute or two, let alone a couple of hours.'

Rhys shrugged his shoulders, 'If I know Giddy, he'll probably fall asleep, and that'll be good for him, won't it?' He waited for their reaction and saw his dad shake his head from side to side, and his mother rolled her eyes.

'Rhys,' she began.

'No, Mam. We're going, straight from work tomorrow evening.' He saw her shoulders droop and he knew that although she didn't like the idea, there was nothing more she could say. He went across to her and put his arm around her waist, 'We'll be fine Mam. Be home on Sunday, before you know it.' Rhys didn't tell her about the clubhouse.

Straightening herself up, she walked towards the stairs, 'Well, then I'd better pack a few things for you, so as you can make a speedy getaway, tomorrow.' Rhys's heart sank, last time he went camping when he was still in the junior school, she had packed his pyjamas. He would have to go through everything before leaving home for sure. Giddy would be merciless in his teasing if there was anything sissy in his gear.

Giddy didn't fare any better in his household. As casually

as possible, at dinner on Thursday evening, he said, 'Me and Rhys are going fishing tomorrow, Mam. We thought we'd take a tent and camp overnight. There's a smashing place about thirty-odd miles away.' As he took a mouthful of mashed potatoes and saw the stricken look on his mother's face, he swallowed quickly and hurried on, 'There's showers, a café, a launderette and a large barn if it should rain.'

'But,' she began.

'Mam, we'll be fine. Back home on Sunday evening, before you know it.'

'Rhys! You mean you're going with that trouble maker?' Giddy opened his mouth and closed it again, anxious to defend his friend, but not wanting to upset his mother further, and kept quiet. 'He's always leading you into trouble. I daren't let you out my sight when he's around.' She took a deep breath, 'No, Idris, I'll not have it. You are not going.' Giddy muttered under his breath. 'What did you say? Don't you dare answer me back.'

Mr Cooper, who had continued eating his dinner, wiped his mouth with the back of his hand, and said, 'That was a lovely chop, my dear.' He smiled across at his wife. 'Now, as I see it, it wasn't that long ago that Rhys was the apple of your eye, my dear. You was always on about how he saved your darling boy's life.'

'That was then, now they both think our boy is back to his old self. Well, he isn't. He's always very tired when he comes in from work – and work, well, that was against my better judgement. And he sleeps nearly all the weekend, trying to catch up on his sleep. That's the best thing for invalids so I make sure he isn't disturbed.'

Mr Cooper shook his head and still smiling, 'All boys do at that age, my dear. I bet Mrs Evans says the same about her lad.'

Turning to Giddy, she pleaded, 'Please don't go, lad. I shall be in a state of nerves the whole time until you're safely back.'

Giddy pushed back his chair and went across to his mother. Putting his hands on her shoulders and kissing the top of her head, he quietly said, 'Shut up, Mam. I'll take great care, but it's time everything was back to normal.'

'What do you mean, normal?'

'Like you swiping me with the towel, when I'm cheeky, or grumbling about the state of my working clothes.' He sighed, 'Please Mam, let's just all be as we were.' He moved towards, the door. 'Now I'm going to put a few things together, so that we don't have to hang around tomorrow night. The sooner we get there, the easier it will be to get settled in.'

He looked back at her and saw she was looking down at her clasped hands in her lap.

'Aw, Mam, give over. I'll be fine, you'll see.'

She lifted her head and smiled at him. 'Leave the packing, I'll do it for you in the morning, love,' was all she said, and he gave a big sigh of relief. Giddy did not mention the clubhouse.

Friday night, and when Giddy went to get his gear he was dismayed to see a suitcase on his bed. With a heavy heart, he opened it and wasn't surprised to see its contents. Four pairs of socks, he removed two, four tee shirts, two jeans, his suit. The suit! Whatever for, he wondered. It was only bought for a job interview, and he never got the job anyway. There was a raincoat and an oversized woollen jumper. And handker-chiefs, extra blankets! The last, and unnecessary in his opinion, was a first aid kit. Not only did it contain the usual plasters and ointments, but there was cough medicine, embrocation for sprains, paracetamol, throat pastilles and a list of telephone numbers for doctors, dentists and hospitals. Quickly, he shoved what he thought was actually essential into a plastic bag, and hid the rest under the bed covers. He would be long gone before anyone found out.

When Rhys arrived to collect Giddy on Friday evening, he saw that Mrs Cooper was fussing over Giddy and trying to hold her tongue. 'You take care now,' she chided, 'don't get into any sort of trouble.'

'Don't worry Mam, it's only thirty or so miles away. Rhys will get me home before you can say, Jack Robinson.' He turned to Rhys who knew without a doubt that the site was more like sixty-five miles away. 'That's right, isn't it, Rhys?'

Picking up one of Giddy's overfull carrier bags, he replied, 'Well, perhaps a bit more than thirty miles, but I'll watch out for him, Mrs Cooper you can bank on it.' Both lads then made for the door as quickly as possible, strapped the bags onto the already full panniers, and began their journey. It was getting dark when they finally arrived at the site, that was surrounded by fields where sheep were grazing. There was plenty of space available but it was Giddy who suggested they make camp near the river, well away from the other campers.

The tent was up, and they had feasted on two bottles of beer Em had hidden in the sleeping bags, and Giddy's mother had packed a couple of sausage rolls and a packet of jam tarts. They kept on their vests and underpants and were just about to settle down to sleep, when Giddy decided to take a look outside.

'What you up to now?' asked Rhys irritable as he snuggled down. 'Come on, get into your sack, you can look around tomorrow.'

'Just a minute,' came the reply. Giddy returned and climbed into his sleeping bag. 'Just thought I'd make sure there were no horses in the field.'

'What made you do that for heaven's sake?'

'Remember when we were kids and went camping, and we heard things go bump in the night?'

'Yes, and you told me it was the witch, Canrig and that she ate little children. Nearly frightened me to death.'

Giddy laughed, 'Well if she calls tonight, I hope she's about sixteen or so and I'll invite her in, I promise.'

Rhys threw a trainer at him as he asked, 'So what about the horses then?'

'Remember, they woke us and we found they had eaten our breakfast.'

'Well there's no animals in the field here, so go to sleep.' As Rhys pulled the bag over is head, he mumbled, 'Good night.'

It was around four o'clock when Giddy shook Rhys awake. 'Rhys, Rhys,' he whispered. 'Are you awake?'

There was a big sigh from Rhys. 'What's up? You feeling ill or something?'

'No, listen. Can you here it?'

'I can hear some bleating, that's what sheep do,' he answered wearily.

'Well, this one's been bleating for hours and hours and keeping me awake. There's something wrong with it, I'm sure.'

'It's the middle of the night, and it's probably nothing. Anyway, it's too dark to do anything about anything at the moment. For heaven's sake, shut up and let me have some sleep, even if you can't.'

It was around six in the morning when Rhys woke up and cheerfully called across to his friend, 'Come on, let's get moving. The clubhouse opens for breakfast at seven.'

It was a very weary Giddy who answered, That poor creature has been going on all night, and what's more, I think there are two of them.'

'Get dressed, we'll have a look to satisfy you, then I'm off for my brekkie.'

Rhys stepped outside and stretched his arms skywards as he looked around. He was surprised to see, not more than ten yards away from the tent, a distressed ewe, pawing at the ground, who swivelled her head round to him when he called out to Giddy to come and have a look. Rhys noted that Giddy had dressed in yesterday's tee shirt and some new shorts he hadn't seen before.

'Definitely something wrong with her,' Giddy said as he strolled over to her. Peering over into the river he called,

'Come quick, Rhys, there's a lamb in the water.' Together they looked down the bank and saw a lamb tangled in some brambles that just held it from entirely entering the swiftly running water. 'We've got to do something, Rhys. I'll climb down and lift it up to you, okay?' and he immediately began climbing down the bank.

'You idiot!' shouted Rhys. 'Come back. We'll go for help.'

'I'm alright, if we leave it any longer, the poor thing might slip and drown.'

'No it won't. It's fixed fast.' Giddy ignored him and continued to carefully slip and slide down towards the lamb. He stretched out his arm to reach it, and saw the brambles were so entwined in its coat, that he would have to get really close up. Carefully, Giddy eased himself down towards the lamb whose cries were now very few and pitiful. 'Oh, you poor little creature,' he said when he finally reached it. 'Come on, let's get you out of here and back with your mam.' It took Giddy some time to carefully disentangle the brambles from the curly coat, noting all the time that the lamb was getting weaker. At last it was clear, and Giddy shouted up to Rhys, 'Lean over the bank and grab her when I lift her up.'

'I'm ready. Be careful, it's very muddy where you are.'

'Don't worry,' Giddy answered as he tucked he cold wet, animal inside his tee shirt and began to climb. He had nearly reached the top of the bank and was out of breath. 'Ready?' he gasped as the thrust the lamb upwards. As Rhys successfully grabbed the lamb, Giddy's feet lost their grip and he tumbled through blackberry bushes and scraped himself on a couple of rocks as he slid fast down the bank into the water.

Sitting at the edge of the river with the water half way up to his chest, he heard Rhys call out, 'Giddy! Giddy! You alright?'

The water was cold and at the same time very soothing on the multiple scratches he'd collected on his unwelcome descent into the water. 'Yes, I'm fine.'

'How you going to get out?'

Giddy looked along the bank and saw a few yards ahead, that there were some steps that led upwards and led to a gangway where one lone fisherman was casting his line. Giddy got to his feet and despite the buffeting from the swirling waters around his legs, made an unsteady walk to the steps. At the top, Rhys was waiting for him. Giddy looked around, 'Where's the lamb, where is it?'

'Where do you think? It took a good swig from its mother then they both cleared off to the flock over there. Left without a nod or a thank you.'

'Well, of course not, you didn't do anything, did you?'

Rhys was about to retort, but saw his friend was shivering with cold and was worryingly very white. 'Here, mate, get yourself over to the showers and get some hot water over you. I'll fetch you some dry clothes and a towel.' He gave Giddy a gentle shove, 'Go on before you catch your death of cold.'

As Giddy began to hurry across the field, he gave turned and gave a weak grin to Rhys. 'You sound just like my mam.'

After the shower Rhys had got him an enormous breakfast, the sight of which made Giddy declare he couldn't possibly eat that much, but did and he began to look better for it. Back at the tent, Rhys picked up the wet clothes, 'What you going to tell your folks happened?' he asked.

Giddy took his time thinking up an answer. 'I think it's best if I say you pushed me into the river.' He heard Rhys give a gasp. 'Well, I'll explain it was an accident of course.'

Rhys was dumbfounded, he could believe his best friend was going to blame him. 'No you won't, you rat. Tell the truth for once.'

'They won't believe I was that brave and I've got to tell them something.'

'Well think of something else,' was the sharp reply, 'And while you're about it, think up a reason for the scratches on your legs and arms.'

'That's easy, I'll say I fell through the brambles on the way down the bank.'

'And your mam will believe you. You know she blames me for all the stupid things you do. Always has and I've been okay with that, but you've been ill and she'll never forgive me for something I didn't do.'

Giving a shrug, Giddy answered, 'Yes she will. Of course, she will. She thinks you are the best thing since sliced bread.'

Rhys muttered, 'I give up.' And stormed away towards the clubhouse.

It was over an hour before Giddy joined Rhys who had spent the time, firstly thumbing through an old discarded newspaper then met up with a group of bikers from Cardiff, had a few laughs and discussed the merits of each of their own bikes. They also told him of a local motorbike assault course. 'What took you so long?' he asked Giddy.

'Took my gear to the launderette, it's all come out lovely and clean.'

'Well, that's a good start. How are you going to explain the scratches, though? Thought about that?'

'Yep, I'll only wear jeans until they disappear.'

'And what about your arms?'

'Don't worry, I'll not blame you, I'll say a dog chased me or something, and I fell into a blackberry bush. I'll not mention you at all.'

After lunch they both decided to just laze around for the afternoon, mostly sunbathing and both got rather red. They also enjoyed, drinking from the bottle, illicit beer bought from an understanding 'Off Licence' proprietor. For their evening meal, they chose beef burgers and chips, followed by bread and butter pudding, 'Not as good as my mam's,' Giddy remarked, but tucked in nevertheless. They decided to see what was happening in the club that promised evening entertainment. Giddy wasn't keen, 'Mate, I'm knackered, rather have a kip, if you don't mind.'

'Aw, come on. Just for an hour or so.' Giddy shook his

head, but brightened up and agreed to go after Rhys had slyly told him, 'I saw a couple of girls, short skirts and giggling earlier. They might be in there.' They stayed for an hour. The other guests were nearly all of pensioner age, there were a couple of families with under-fives making the most of out-of -term price reductions, but no girls. The entertainment was bingo, with an indifferent caller. Neither of the boys felt inclined to play.

'Right, I'm off,' declared Giddy.

'And me,' As they walked back to their tent in the fading light, they discussed plans for tomorrow. 'How about we try to find that assault course and have a go?'

'Great,' Giddy replied.

'Nothing too daring, Gid. Got to get you home in one piece at least.'

'Ah, home, I suppose we'd better make tracks after lunch.'

'Exactly what I thought.'

After an uneventful night, both were wakened by the sound of heavy rain drumming on the tent. They looked at each in dismay. There would be no excursions of any sort today, instead they would have to pack up in the pouring rain. Both were glum as they dressed and decided not to bother with crossing the field to the washrooms or café, even though the smell of bacon cooking was tempting. Both grumbled as they hastily packed their belongings and took the tent down that billowed around them as they tried to fold it neatly into its container. In the end, they just shoved it in and hoped for the best. Rhys knew that Emlyn would not be pleased.

Rhys insisted on driving and Giddy agreed reluctantly, knowing his friend would not take any silly chances that if he was in charge he might make. 'I'm sick of being wet and cold,' he grumbled. 'Really looking forward to my Sunday dinner and ...'

'Sunday dinner. You'll be lucky, we won't be home much before four.'

'My mam will keep me a dinner, you can bet on it,' was the smug reply, and Rhys, knowing Mrs Cooper, had to agree.

Today, Friday, was the last day of the term at college and there was an awards ceremony in the evening. Rhys had been told the day before that his work on his jewel box warranted commendation and now he was on his way to pick up his certificate. He had showered and dressed in his favourite jeans and short-sleeved cotton shirt. 'My word, you do look smart, even combed your hair,' remarked his mother. 'Meeting your girl afterwards?'

How did she know, Rhys asked himself, then thought it was probably Nan who had told her? 'You never know,' he replied, knowing that his blushing face gave him away. It may be the last chance to put things right, he very much hoped so.

'Leave over, woman, let the lad alone,' said his father as he winked at Rhys.

Helen had passed him by without speaking on a number of occasions and he had resigned himself to having lost her. At the time all he could think about was how ill Giddy was. He wished with all his heart, he had stopped and explained to her why he had so rudely left her standing in the corridor.

He felt a little nervous as he mounted the steps to the stage to receive his certificate and shake the Head's hand, who asked him, 'And what are you going to do with this charming little box?

Rhys mumbled back, 'I had someone in mind, but, well, we'll see who. Probable my mam or nan.'

'Well done, young man, whoever gets this will really appreciate it.' Rhys was more than relieved to return to this seat. More carpenter apprentices followed, then the engineering department awards were announced. Rhys was pleased to hear that Helen had come top of her year and he watched her beam as she accepted the silver cup as the head remarked that it was rare for a girl to achieve so much in what was predominantly a male occupation. Rhys inwardly thought if it had been anyone else saying that, they would have got the sharp end of Helen's tongue.

At the end of the evening Rhys, along with others, shook hands, congratulated each other and promised to see each other in September when the college re-opened. Rhys was one of the last to leave. He had been unable to get Helen's attention and admitted to himself, it was now unlikely that there would be any sort of friendship with her. It was getting dark as he walked passed the bicycle sheds on his way to the drive leading to the gates, but stopped when he saw that something was going on. The very stance of the figures suggested some sort of aggression. He assured himself that he would not get involved, but if someone was in trouble well … he wasn't sure what he would do. Quietly he walked towards them, and as he got closer, he was alarmed to see three youths surrounding a girl who had her back to the wall.

One of them was jeering at her. 'Teacher's pet, that's what you are. From the moment you entered the room, we could all see he was very, very interested in you.'

Another voice interrupted, 'I wouldn't be surprised if she was sleeping with him, getting those sort of marks.'

'Yes, a favour returned. You do know he is married?' questioned the third.

At first glance, Rhys couldn't see clearly who the trembling girl was, but within an instant he saw it was Helen – and he was angry, especially when he saw one of the boys stepping closer to her, saying at the same time, 'Well, I'm just as good as he is. What about trying me out?'

How dare anybody speak to a girl, his girl, like that? Rhys thought.

Momentarily, Rhys didn't know what to do. He knew that if Giddy was with him, he wouldn't have hesitated but would have taken on the three of them with his arms flailing in the air as he thumped them. But he was on his own, and knew he had to do something. Then remembered watching a television drama where the villain said. 'Create a diversion.' But what? There was no time to think things through, but suddenly Rhys thrust himself between the surprised lads, reached Helen's side and pulled her arm through his.

'Sorry I'm, late, Mr Spencer wanted a word, wanted to personally say how pleased he was with my work, and so ... Well, here I am at last.' He turned to the group, 'Been looking after my girl? Thanks.' There was muttering from the lads, and as they turned away, he said, 'Come on, Helen. Your dad will be waiting. You know what he's like if you're late.' Addressing the gang, he added with a rueful laugh, 'I tell you now, you don't want to ever cross her dad.'

Rhys began to lead Helen away and the others went off in the opposite direction. Helen, tried to pull her arm away from him, 'Leave it there, I like it, sort of cosy.'

He felt her relax, then she said in a soft voice, 'Thank you, Rhys, I don't know what would have happened if you hadn't come. I was really scared. I could have thumped one, but had no chance with three of them.'

'They were miffed that you came top, damaged their ego or something, I reckon.'

'Serves them right, always mucking about in the workshop.' She paused for a moment then went on, 'I think I once called you a pervert. I'm really sorry, but the way the lads behave sometimes in the workshop, really cheeses me off.'

Rhys, gave a quiet chuckle, 'Yes, you did, but I'll forgive you this time.'

They walked on in silence for a few moments, then she said, 'It was a great idea, pretending you're my boyfriend.'

'Well, that's all I could think of at the time as, like you, there's no way, I could have tackled three of them.' He smiled down at her upturned face, 'I'm not that brave. Besides, for a long time, I've thought of you as my girlfriend.'

'They were really awful. That bit about my dad, by the way,

was so, so true.'

'Really?' I hope not Rhys thought, I want to go out with you with no more trouble. An overprotective father might be difficult.

'I've been pretty rotten to you, haven't I? I could tell you were sorry, but, well, as you now know, I can be very stubborn.' She hesitated, 'I heard about your friend and realised you were upset, but then, well you know, it's difficult to ...'

'Oh, let's forget it,' he interjected. 'Come on, I'll see you home.'

'Rhys,' began Helen, 'my dad's not really fierce, he's just looking out for me.'

'Well, perhaps, he'll let me share that job,' he replied as he pulled her closer.

They were nearly at her house when he stopped and removed her arm from his. Reaching inside his jacket, he proudly said, 'Here, I made this for you, my first apprenticeship assignment.' Then added, 'It's a jewel or keepsake box. I hope you like it.'

He watched her caress the silky finish of the wooden gift, then smile as she said, 'It's beautiful. Thank you. I'll treasure it always.'

They had reached the front garden gate and stopped for a moment. Rhys began, 'Can I ... Will you ...' With some dismay, he suddenly stopped, 'Oh, L...Lord,' he stuttered, 'I forgot. I mean, well, have you got a boyfriend, Helen or someone special?' He held his breath, waiting for her answer, but dreading it as well.

'Boyfriend?' she queried. 'What makes you think that for goodness' sake?'

Rhys was delighted, it was possible that she didn't have a fella.

'Oh,' he said casually, 'I saw you once with a lad, in the village post office. It looked as if ...'

'When?'

'Ages ago, well about five or six months.'

Helen gave a little chuckle, 'I know when you mean. Rather handsome, wasn't he?' she teased. Rhys shrugged as if he didn't care.

'Well, if you must know, it was my cousin Colin, came for a visit from Shrewsbury and we decided on some treats while we watched the telly.'

Rhys gave an inward sigh of relief, and asked, 'Shall I see you tomorrow?' He stopped for a moment then hurried on, 'We could go to the pictures or bowling if you like.' The front door opened and he could see a giant of a man framed in the light. He thought to himself, yes I was right. I'd protect any beautiful daughter of mine too.

Helen, laughed, 'Hi Dad,' she called out. 'Just coming. This is Rhys, he brought me home.'

'Good lad,' Rhys heard him say. 'Say goodnight, lass and get yourself indoors.'

'See you tomorrow,' she whispered to Rhys. Then added, 'And don't bring that awful bike!'

Rhys was surprised by her remark, 'What do you mean?'

'I'm nearly a qualified engineer,' she retorted, 'and I wouldn't be seen dead on that.'

'I'll probably be late then, 'cos I'll have to walk.'

Helen waved her hand airily as she entered her house, and laughed as she said, 'Goodnight, Rhys. See you.'

'See you tomorrow,' he replied. The last bus to his village was due but Rhys was grinning to himself as he ran to the bus stop. It was sometime later, whilst eating the sandwich his mother had left out for his supper, that it occurred to him he would have to explain to Giddy tomorrow about a change in plans. I'll tell him, I'll make it up to him on Sunday, that might just work, he told himself.

THE END

Acknowledgements

Kevin Moloney for the delightful tales of how he, with his brother, teased their father.

Illustrations although mostly by the author, some were inspired by two good friends, David Ferris d'ced artist and poet, and Noel Terry, d'ced also an artist and writer.

Jenny Hunt for her diligence in finding what I missed.

My two sons, Derek who shared and guided me through his apprenticeship experiences. And Ray, who thinks Rhys and Giddy are his best friends so encourages me to write more and more of their adventures. He is already feeding me ideas for a further book in the series. Both give me their unstinting support.

Anne and John Samson at TSL Publications, who have again given me their unstinting support and encouragement.

BOOKS BY BEATRICE

Rhys series

1. Training a Greyhound and Other Troubles
2. Urgent! Pocket Money Required
3. Disasters and Delights of Family Celebrations
4. Enormous Responsibilities
5. The Sometimes Society
6. When Rhys Fell Out a Tree
7. A Question of Girls

Towing Path Tales

1. Towing Path Tales
2. More Towing Path Tales
3. A Particular Year

Adult

1. A Man from the North
2. Archie's Children
3. Elusive Destiny
4. Facts, Folklore and Feasts of Christmas (non-fiction)
5. Retired? You must be joking

Plays

1. A Certain Monday
2. Connie's Lovely Boy
3. From Commoner to Coronet
4. Governed by Magpies
5. In Less than Ten Minutes
6. Plays for Young Actors

www.ingramcontent.com/pod-product-compliance
Lightning Source LLC
Chambersburg PA
CBHW060134260626
47160CB00005B/2105